PENGUIN BOOKS
THE WEDDING PHOTOGRAPHER

Sakshama Puri Dhariwal was born in Delhi and brought up in the era of 1990s' Bollywood music. She has an MBA in marketing from S.P. Jain Institute of Management and Research, Mumbai, and has worked as a brand manager for e-commerce, media and telecom companies. Sakshama currently lives in San Francisco with her husband. *The Wedding Photographer* is her first novel.

D1601544

For my parents, Meenoo and Atul Puri,
because by the time you introduced me to cable TV,
it was too late.
I had already fallen in love with books.

THE
WEDDING
PHOTOGRAPHER

PART ONE
THE FLIGHT

Hour 1

This was the worst flight of Risha Kohli's life.

Scratch that. This was most likely the worst *day* of her life, even though it hadn't started out that way. Despite being unable to check-in online the night before, Risha had managed to secure an aisle seat on a seventeen-hour flight from Los Angeles to New Delhi. The thought of spending those many hours squashed between two fat desi uncles, travelling from 'Amreeka' to *'mera desh meri mitti'* had kept her up all night. Which is why Risha nearly passed out with relief upon discovering that the alphabet next to her seat number corresponded with an aisle seat. Imagine her pleasant surprise when she learnt that her seat number was, in fact, the exact same as her bra size. Best day ever, right?

Wrong.

Because Risha was seated next to a little boy with an inability to 'hold it'. For the fourth time in an hour and fifteen minutes, the kid turned to his mother. 'Mummy, I want to toilet.'

'No, Bunty,' his mother responded without looking away from the tiny screen in front of her. 'Just now only you went, you can't be going again *itni jaldi*. Watch your cartoon *chup-chaap*.'

'But I did *su-su* last time, now I want to potty,' Bunty said urgently.

Risha unbuckled her seat belt with a pre-emptive sigh. So much for getting some desperately needed sleep on the coveted aisle seat.

Bunty's mother had the decency to look apologetic. 'Sorry, behenji, hope you are not minding again and again we are disturbing you.'

Risha tried to smile, but it came out as a grimace. 'It's okay.'

Bunty practically leapt over Risha, one hand already unzipping his Ben10 pants as he sprinted to the toilet with his mother in tow. Risha walked towards the cabin crew seats and spotted an Indian flight attendant wearing the reddest lipstick she had ever seen. Glancing at the woman's name tag, she put on her most sororal smile. 'Kritika, I'm so sorry for the trouble, but is there a vacant seat you can move me to?'

In a phony British accent, Kritika replied, 'I'm so sorry, love. The flight is full.'

'I understand, but I'm sitting next to this little kid and—'

She cut Risha off with a sugary smile. 'I'm so sorry, love. The flight is full.'

Risha gritted her teeth. 'Yes, but—'

With another pretentious smile, Kritika gestured to her blond colleague. 'Connor and I really must get on with the service, love. Now, if you would please excuse us?'

Connor shot Risha a sympathetic look before following Kritika.

'*Bitch*ika,' Risha muttered under her breath, heading back to her seat.

Only sixteen hours to go, she told herself. You can survive this.

It wouldn't be so bad if she wasn't already under-slept. Kabir was right, the direct flight from LA to Delhi was a bad idea. 'Another day won't make a difference,' he had assured her. 'I have things under control here.' But Risha didn't want to push him, because this trip, and photography in general, was her personal project. It had nothing to do with her 'real' job as assistant editor, *Delhi Today*, the entertainment and lifestyle supplement of *News Today*. And as her boss, Kabir Bose had no reason to go easy on her.

Risha's friend, Nidhi, had overheard Kabir telling Sukhdeep Pal Singh Baweja, the sports editor, that Risha was the 'best journo *News Today* ever had the honour of employing, and the newspaper would surely shut down without her'. Like most marketing people, Nidhi had a tendency to exaggerate.

Kabir hadn't exactly deified Risha, as Nidhi claimed, but he *had* excluded her name from an explosive tirade targeted at the rest of his team. Apparently, what Kabir had *really* said, was, 'How can I put together a forty-eight-page supplement when I'm short of three reporters, one designer, and constantly have to babysit two of the most incompetent interns ever? How did these people get their journalism degrees without learning to spell simple words like "connoisseur" and "faux pas"? The other day, I heard one of the interns ask Risha what "tay-tay a tay-tay" means. Risha looked appalled at first, then explained that a "tête-à-tête" is a private chit-chat. At least one person out of eight can pronounce basic words, Sukhi!'

Sukhi, under the influence of Karl Marx and Johnny Walker, though probably not in that order, had told Kabir to 'stop being an elitist bastard and come to terms with the fact that the vocabulary of an average *NT* reader consists of only eleven eight-letter words'. Then, only for effect, he added, 'Just because you live in Friends Colony and throw random French words into your weekly column doesn't mean that you can deny others the bloody joie de vivre associated with writing!'

Nidhi didn't know what happened after that because she ran off to take a phone call—something she'd been doing a lot since her recent marriage to cricketer Vikram Walia. But if Risha had to guess, Kabir was probably furious at Sukhi's hypocrisy. Because when it came to venting about the ineptitude of his own sports writers, Sukhi was a known cribber. And on an unrelated note, he was also a borderline alcoholic, with serious anger issues. Risha suspected the only reason editor-in-chief Jay Soman humoured Sukhi was because of his connections in the BCCI. Sukhi had played a few international matches in his time, but due to a severe shoulder injury, his cricket career had come to a premature end.

'The only reason he's so bitter and angry all the time is because his dream of becoming the next Navjyot Singh Sidhu was shattered,' Nidhi hypothesized. 'Can you imagine what the world would look like if, in addition to Sidhu-isms, we also had to put up with Sukhi-isms?' Nidhi had asked while driving Risha to the Delhi airport.

'God forbid.' Risha shuddered at the thought.

'Is your lover boy okay with you taking more days off after returning from LA?' Nidhi asked.

'Real mature. Just because Kabir is supportive of my photography, doesn't make him my "lover boy".'

'Of course he's supportive, like he has a choice! You're making five times what our shitty jobs at *NT* pay us.'

'If you hate your job so much, why don't you just quit?'

'As soon as Vikram is back from the Australia tour, I'm going to resign.'

'You would be so much happier doing the NGO thing full time.'

'The NGO "thing"? You're so articulate; ever considered a career in journalism?' Nidhi quipped.

'Hilarious.'

'And what do you mean if *I* hate my job? *You* hate yours too, don't you?'

Risha shrugged. 'I like writing, just not about boring society parties. Actually, Kabir has been quite understanding about that, too. I've basically transitioned to Health & Lifestyle, and he's making Charu and the interns work the Page 3 beat. *And* he has promised me a weekly photo essay as soon as the team is back to its full strength.'

Nidhi's green eyes flashed with interest. 'He is *so* in love with you.'

'No, he's not.'

'You should totally date him,' Nidhi insisted. 'He's exactly like Rahul Khanna in *Wake Up Sid*—suave, sophisticated and super hot.'

'Don't forget "pseudo"! And Konkana dumps Rahul Khanna for Ranbir Kapoor. Also, you're married—does Vikram know that you have a crush on my boss?' Risha asked, well aware that Nidhi had eyes only for her drop-dead gorgeous husband.

Just like half the country's population.

'I'm just being objective. Until you find Ranbir, you should totally date Rahul. I mean, Kabir.'

'I will take your advice into consideration. Not.'

'If you're not going to date him, you have zero incentive to work at *NT*. Honestly, with the kind of money you're making per wedding, you could do photography full time. The fact that you're also passionate about it is a bonus.'

'I'm just multitasking as long as I can,' Risha said.

'And the monthly pay check doesn't hurt either,' Nidhi pointed out.

'Yes, unfortunately, some of us aren't married to the richest cricketer in the world.'

'Hey! I never—' Nidhi's retort was interrupted by her phone and she gave Risha a sheepish grin. 'Speak of the devil.'

Risha smiled and turned her face to the window, allowing Nidhi a modicum of privacy to speak with her husband.

In a way, Risha owed her success at wedding photography to Nidhi and Vikram. She was the photographer at their wedding, and had posted a few candid shots on her blog. Even though there weren't too many close-ups of Vikram, Nidhi had been recognized by a few fans, causing the photos to go viral. Risha had received dozens of calls after that, mostly from crazy fans, but a few legitimate queries as well.

So when Risha asked her first client, Ridhima Jaipuria, for one lakh rupees, and wondered if she had overpriced her services, Nidhi banned her from negotiating costs with anyone. 'Are you crazy? Any amateur can make a lakh! You shot *Vikram Walia's wedding*!'

Risha gave her friend an amused smile. 'How is it that you absolutely refuse to drop Vikram's name even to get a table at a restaurant, but have no qualms about stooping to the level of a middle-class Delhite when it comes to me?'

Nidhi looked at Risha as if she were mad. 'Because you're my best friend, but also because you're the most talented photographer I know. And hello, if I need a table at a restaurant, I simply flash my press card!'

Nidhi had called back Ridhima Jaipuria, claiming to be Risha's manager, and clarified that one lakh meant one lakh *per day*, and for four days it would amount to four lakhs *plus* service tax. Ridhima had agreed immediately, as if one lakh or four lakhs was all the same to her. She then dropped her voice to a conspiratorial whisper. 'Did she really shoot Vikram Walia's wedding?'

Nidhi scoffed at that. 'Of course, she did.'

'Is it true that his wife is a total south Delhi snob?'

There was a long pause before Nidhi responded, 'She can be.' And with that, she slammed the phone on the daughter of the thirteenth richest man in India.

In addition to being the sixth wedding Risha had shot, the LA wedding was her very first overseas assignment. Over the course of the week, Risha had done the pre-wedding shoot, followed by the whole wedding shebang. The wedding was larger, grander and more exhausting than any other she had ever shot.

Add three hours of sleep a day for a week to a non-stop seventeen-hour flight and a seat next to a compulsive toilet goer, and what do you get? Worst day ever.

Bunty poked his skinny finger into Risha's thigh. 'Aunty, *thoda* side.'

Hoping he had washed his hands, Risha gave him a smile. 'I'm only a few years older than you. At least call me didi, yaar!'

Bunty giggled as he slid into his seat. 'You called me "yaar". That means I'm your boyfriend!'

Risha frowned. 'No, you're not.'

'Do you have a boyfriend?'

Risha glowered at him. 'Watch your cartoon chup-chaap.'

The last thing she wanted to do was to discuss her love life, or lack thereof, with a nine-year-old.

Bunty's mother scowled at him. 'Bunty, don't do *badtameezi* or I will tell air hostess aunty to drop you at the next stop.'

Bunty's eyes widened and his lips quivered with fear. Risha smothered a laugh. Served the little monster right.

Realizing that she wouldn't be getting much sleep next to Mr Su-su Potty, Risha stood up and reached into the overhead bin for her laptop.

Hour 3

Risha plugged her memory card into her laptop, grumbling to herself. Nidhi called this her 'post-partum depression phase', sifting through thousands of photos for the first cut selection. Unlike traditional wedding photographers, Risha didn't believe in sending her clients thousands of photos to choose from. She spent a substantial amount of time on a thorough quality check. She painstakingly looked through each image, discarding the ones with poor lighting or resolution, cluttered frames and, most importantly, the non-candid images or 'posers'. Most clients had a regular photographer to cater to requests such as '*Hamare kitty party group ki ek photo lena*'; they didn't need Risha for that.

Risha gulped down her lukewarm coffee, and started with the obvious thumbnails.

Select, delete. Select, delete.

If Risha ever quit her job to do photography full time, the first thing she would do would be to hire an assistant for this specific task. She loved taking photos and even enjoyed working on the album design, but the tedium of going through each and every image was something she could do without.

One particular image caught her eye and she zoomed in on it. It was a photo of the bride's father during the *vidaai*. His eyes glimmered with unshed tears and his lips were pursed together to suppress the inevitable breakdown. Just looking at the emotion captured in the image gave Risha goosebumps. It was photos like these that made her love wedding photography so much.

Risha's faraway smile was interrupted by an elbow jammed into her ribs.

'He is your boyfriend, na?' Bunty giggled.

She shot Bunty an angry glare that made him jump in his seat, knocking over his juice box and sending a spray of sticky orange juice all over her laptop.

Risha froze. Bunty's mother stared at Risha in horror. 'Behenji, I am raylee raylee sorry.'

She whacked Bunty on the head and said in a menacing tone, 'Bunty, *ab tu dekh* what I will do with you. I will throw you out from this window and you will have to reach Delhi on your own!'

The threat sounded legit to Risha. A moment later, it was confirmed that Bunty had bought it too, because his fear-stricken bowels finally caved in. And just like that, Bunty *went* in his seat.

Hour 5

'Are you kidding me, Kritika?' Risha exploded. 'A boy just pooped in the seat next to mine! Do you seriously expect me to spend the next twelve hours sitting there?'

'I'm so sorry, love—'

'Yes, I know. "The flight is full." You have to do *something*. I've been sitting there patiently for the last two hours, but I just can't take it any more. I'll sit anywhere else. ANYWHERE!' Risha said in exasperation. Whatever happened to *'ek Hindustani hi ek Hindustani ke kaam aa sakta hai'*? Way to set false expectations, *DDLJ*.

Risha turned to Connor for help, but he just shrugged.

Kritika arched a perfectly shaped brow. 'You'll sit anywhere?'

'Yes!' Risha nodded.

'Last row?'

'Sure!' Risha agreed with relief.

'Non-reclining?'

'Absolutely!'

'Next to the toilet?' Kritika asked.

'I'm already sitting next to the toilet. Get it?' Risha winked.

Kritika gave her a blank look, then broke into her trademark faux grin. 'I'm so sorry, love. The flight is full.' Then she whipped around and walked off.

Risha stared after Kritika, puzzled. Was this woman a robot trapped in a human's body? Risha turned to Connor with a helpless look. 'What just happened?'

'What happened,' Connor said, taking a step closer to her, 'is that a seat just opened up in business class.'

Risha was caught off guard by his sudden proximity, but the words 'business class' made her ears perk up. She tossed her long brown hair behind her shoulder and tipped her head innocently. 'What do you mean?'

'Kritika is always a cow to girls who are prettier than her,' he said with a flattering smile.

Risha giggled. Or she *hoped* it was a giggle. Nidhi always said Risha's laugh was like a Punjabi man's— loud, hearty and interspersed with snorts. Risha prayed this laugh had sounded more like Aishwarya Rai and less like Kangana Ranaut.

'The airline has a strict guideline about broken TV screens,' Connor explained, taking another step towards Risha. He was now standing a mere six inches from Risha and she was beginning to feel quite uneasy. Or maybe it was the garlic on his breath that was making her nauseated.

Risha considered herself fairly inept at the art of flirting, so she racked her brain for the contents of Kabir's latest weekly column titled 'Flirt Your Way to Success: 5 Handy Tips'.

She had already done the hair-tossing and giggling, what else was left? Ah, the slouching! The article had mentioned that men like women who *literally* look up to them, because apparently it gives them a faux sense of power. At 5'8", Risha was taller than most Indian men—and definitely this petite British man—so she bent her knees to appear shorter. 'Go on.'

Connor's smile widened. 'On any flight longer than four hours, if the TV screen is not working, the passenger is entitled to a seat change. And if there is no seat available in the passenger's class, the passenger is entitled to an upgrade.'

Risha looked puzzled. 'But my TV screen—'

'*Isn't* working. I know, love. Give me a few minutes and I'll arrange for you to move up a few seats.' He winked. 'Terms and conditions apply.'

Risha frowned. 'What terms and conditions?'

He straightened and said nervously, 'Uh, your phone number? So I can ring you in Delhi, and maybe we can get a drink?'

Wait, what? All she had to do was give this guy a fake number and she could get upgraded to business class? She had given out fake numbers to persistent guys at weddings more times than she could count. It was so much easier than going through the whole 'I'm not interested' routine.

'Of course,' Risha said with a demure smile. 'Why don't you come by business class in a bit and I'll feed it into your phone?'

'Done.'

Hour 6

From: Risha Kohli <risha.kohli@newstoday.in>
To: Nidhi Marwah <nidhi.marwah@newstoday.in>
Subject: Best day ever

Guess where I am right now?

Nidhi's response came immediately:

Based on the subject of your email and the number of hours you've been airborne, I've narrowed it down to two possibilities:

(1) Your flight had to make an emergency landing at a five-star resort where you are using the free Wi-Fi while you wait to start a three-hour spa therapy (because I can't imagine you ever paying for Wi-Fi. Yeah, yeah, it's the principle of the thing, blah blah, who cares?)

(2) You got upgraded to business/first class and you're using the free in-flight Wi-Fi

I kinda hope it's the first one, so you can catch some sleep before—oh, I don't know—the biggest wedding of the century?

Risha scoffed and wrote back:

Obviously, it's (2). As if I would ever waste three hours of my life at a spa. Boring.
Long story, but yes, I got upgraded to business class. Also, the Khanna–Singhal wedding is hardly the 'biggest wedding of the century'. You're thinking Ranbir–Kat (if they hadn't split up).

Nidhi responded:

For a person who claims to dislike her job, you sure use a lot of Bollywood references.

Fine, it may not be the biggest wedding of the century, but two relatively famous people are marrying each other and, in case you've forgotten, the festivities are four days long. So stop emailing me and get some sleep.

Yeah right, Risha thought as she typed her reply:

There's *no* way I'm going to waste my first (and probably last) business class experience sleeping.
Did you know the seats recline all the way? As in, they turn into a bed! And they make fancy cocktails for you with little umbrellas in them. I'm going to ask for single malt with an umbrella just because I *can*. I'm guessing this is what Air Force One is like. I feel like the most powerful person in the world. I can never travel economy again.

Nidhi's response was instant and concerned:

Whoa! How much caffeine have you consumed?

Risha replied:

Not much. Two lattes and a Diet Coke.
Not much.
Listen, there's a bunch of buttons here but I don't know what they do. I got upgraded mid-flight so I missed the business class orientation programme. Oh wait, I'll just use the free Wi-Fi to google it.

Nidhi wrote back:

I don't think they have an 'orientation programme', Rish.

Anyway, since you have a hundred more hours of flight time and you refuse to sleep, I'm attaching the most recent set of matrimonial ads from your parents. Sorry I opened the package, but it's been sitting here for a week and I was tempted to see if any of the guys are worth meeting. I regret to inform you, they are not.

PS: God forbid your parents ever discover matrimonial websites.

Attachment: [scan]punjabiboys.jpg

News Today courier log
Sender's name: Dr A.K. Kohli, Amritsar
Receiver's name: Risha Kohli, New Delhi
Date of receipt: Feb 17, 2016
Time stamp: 12:17 PM

> Well-settled doctor from Amritsar (29, 5'8", fair, handsome, teetotaller) seeks upper-caste, well-educated, stylish, open-minded, slim girl. Only demand is girl should know cooking. Contact: balleboy007@rediffmail.com

Ignoring the ads, Risha wrote:

> You know how they have those windows in
> limousines between the driver and the passengers?
> They have them in business class too! Most of the
> adjacent seats face each other and the dividers are
> supposed to ensure privacy. Except, in a limo they
> separate the rich from the poor, and in business
> class they separate the rich from the rich.
> Btw, I just rolled down the divider by mistake and
> the guy on the other side is reading *News Today*!
> But he's reading the main paper, not *Delhi Today*. I
> can read the front page from here and I've already
> spotted three typos. If I can see three typos from
> two feet away, you think our readers will miss them?
> P.S. God forbid my parents ever discover the Internet.

Nidhi replied:

> Frankly, the vocabulary of *NT* readers rivals most six-
> year-olds. I just checked with the marketing insights

manager, and according to her, in the last few focus groups one thing readers repeatedly asked for was 'more SMS lingo'. I hardly think you need to worry about typos.

Why don't you try talking to the guy next to you instead of reading the front page, dummy?

Risha rolled her eyes and typed:

I refuse to talk to a random stranger. What if he's a murderer? I can't see his face behind the *NT* masthead but he's wearing a Rolex. You know how I feel about expensive watches.

Nidhi's response was defensive:

Hey, Vikram has a Rolex! Even though he got it for endorsing the brand. Stop being judgy. Just because you wear an orange watch, doesn't mean the rest of us shouldn't—oh, what the hell, I love your watch. Especially the adorable little panda on the minute hand!

And hello, I seriously doubt a guy flying business class is a murderer. Although he could've been upgraded from economy, just like you.

Risha addressed the most important part of the email:

I can't believe I'm friends with someone who doesn't know that the 'adorable little panda' is Po from *Kung Fu Panda*.

Hour 8

Arjun Khanna despised journalists.

Most of them were dishonest, duplicitous and generally spineless. Two days ago, Arjun had spent half an hour on the phone with Vandana Kumar, the business editor of *News Today*. The conversation had resulted in a typo-ridden article that contained nothing substantial about the range of affordable homes Arjun had just launched in the national capital region.

NCR was swarming with young working professionals, most of them willing to stretch their budget to afford the lifestyle they aspired for. Instead of delineating Khanna Developers' strategy to target these young professionals, the article went on ad nauseam about the company's rich heritage and how the legendary Arvind Khanna had pioneered high-end luxury condos in India. It was sycophantic garbage meant to suck up to his father.

While it was factually correct, the newspaper article did not serve Arjun's purpose. The entire objective of the interview was to promote affordable housing, a segment his company had recently entered through the launch of their new residential towers 'Casa Gurgaon', by Khanna Developers. If anything, the article should have included something about the company's branding challenge of creating an identity that was premium without being luxury. Arjun's marketing team had spent several months developing a brand that borrowed credibility from the Khanna name without letting it overshadow Casa Gurgaon's core essence—affordability.

But all Vandana had taken out of their thirty-minute conversation was the following quote: 'From building

Lego blocks to luxury condos, my dad has taught me everything I know. He's my hero.'

The article was accompanied by a photograph of Arjun outside Casa Gurgaon, cutting a red ribbon with a large pair of inaugural scissors. He scowled as he discovered an entire paragraph detailing his physical appearance.

'Arjun Khanna, along with Internet mogul and brother-in-law-to-be Rohan Singhal, recently made *NT*'s list of '30 Hottest CEOs Under 30'. An innately private person (much to the chagrin of his PR team), the 6'2" fitness enthusiast seldom makes appearances at social events or Bollywood parties. Last year, the debonair businessman attended cricketer Vikram Walia's star-studded wedding bash, and more recently he was spotted finishing the Mumbai Marathon. Since this interview was conducted telephonically, this journalist was denied the pleasure of seeing the dashing real estate tycoon in person.'

Was this seriously one of India's largest read dailies, he thought with disgust. And if so, why did its readers care about how tall he was, or whose wedding he attended? He was better off being an anonymous associate in a New York investment bank than being a famous CEO back home.

Arjun tossed the newspaper aside impatiently and reached for his laptop, mentally typing out a stinker to his director of corporate communications. He was done with these trashy publications. In fact, he was done with the press altogether. Maybe Dad should handle these guys, Arjun thought grimly. But the PR team insisted on showcasing twenty-nine-year-old Arjun as the new face of Khanna Developers instead of its fifty-six-year-old founder, Arvind.

Four years ago, Arjun had given up his investment banking job in New York and moved back home after his father's heart attack. In the interest of his father's health, Arjun had tried to limit his involvement in the company to ceremonial tasks, and the senior Khanna had welcomed the reprieve. So letting Arvind handle something as critical and high-intensity as PR was out of the question. Although, Arjun thought with amusement, his father didn't exactly think of public relations as 'work'. Arvind Khanna's famous combination of charm and humour often had reporters eating out of the palm of his hand. If only Arjun had inherited his father's people skills in addition to his business acumen.

Arjun's email alert sounded and he smiled at the pleasant interruption, an email from his sister. Chinky—her given name was Nitisha, though Arjun hadn't called her that in years—was by far the calmest bride Arjun had seen, but their mother's recent shenanigans were wreaking havoc on Chinky's tranquil temperament. A few months ago, Amrita Khanna had joined the Science of Living (SoL), an organization run by Sri Sri Priye Guru Ma, formerly known as Priya Sinha, Miss South Delhi 1989. Apparently, Amrita was quite adamant about having a SoL satsang to ensure a *shubh* beginning to the wedding festivities.

'Dear Bhai, is it okay if we don't invite Mom to the wedding?' the email began, and then went on to make a compelling argument for institutionalizing their mother 'even if we have to keep it a secret from the press'. The email ended with an attached draft of the invite their mother had proposed for the satsang.

WITH HER AUGUST PRESENCE

Sri Sri Priye Guru Ma

WILL GRACE THE SCIENCE OF LIVING SATSANG
TO INITIATE THE WEDDING FESTIVITIES OF

Nitisha

DAUGHTER OF AMY AND ARVIND KHANNA

&

Rohan

SON OF VINITA AND VIJAY SINGHAL

AT 5 P.M. ON TUESDAY, 23 FEBRUARY 2016
FOLLOWED BY PURE VEGETARIAN DINNER

THE SCIENCE OF LIVING ASHRAM
LODHI ROAD, NEW DELHI

From: Arjun Khanna <ceo@khannadevelopers.com>
To: Nitisha Khanna <nitisha@khudai.com>
Subject: Re: Satsang

Chinky,

I think Priye Ma's name is not prominent enough. We can definitely increase the font size by a couple of points.
Also, who is Amy?

Nitisha's frustration was evident in her response:

Very funny.
Mom insists on being called Amy because, according to Priye Ma, the name is 'closer to the Pentagon of Perfection'. And Mom thinks it's 'cuter'.
What time does your flight land? Please get here asap and handle her, Bhai. I've got enough going on with the wedding prep and I'm also really swamped with work.

Arjun sympathized with his sister:

I have three extra years of experience in the matter, so trust me when I say this: what Amy wants, Amy gets. Save yourself some time and let her do what she likes.
And here's an idea, if you are so swamped with work, why don't you *buy* your wedding outfit from somewhere else instead of designing it yourself? That way you'll have one less outfit to produce in your workshop.

Nitisha's email sounded irate:

> You really don't know anything.
> My wedding lehenga was finalized a month ago,
> including fittings. And even if it wasn't, how would it
> look if I didn't wear Khudai at my *own* wedding. Why
> don't you just live in a DLF building instead of the
> penthouse at Khanna Heights?

Arjun wrote back:

> Yes, I'm thinking of moving to DLF Aralias. Don't tell
> Dad.
> By the way, I need to buy clothes for your wedding.

Nitisha's response was crisp:

> You already did. You're welcome.

Arjun smiled at the last email. Chinky always had his
back. He stood up and walked towards the galley snack
bar to pick up more water bottles. Staying hydrated was
the first step to beating jet lag, and Arjun needed all the
help he could get.

Arjun had just spent the last four days getting wasted
at the extended bachelor party of his former roommate,
Karan, along with two of their close friends, Ali and
Angad. Technically, they had only spent the first night in
Vegas, drinking and gambling into the wee hours of the
morning. On the second night, Karan had the brilliant
idea of doing a road trip to Mexico.

And since all stupid ideas are born after five drinks,
the guys had spent thirty hours on the road, and upon

reaching Mexico, squandered the night drinking and gambling—the reason, Arjun pointed out, they had picked Vegas in the first place.

'But then we would never have seen Mexico, bro!' Karan justified, before he proceeded to beat Arjun in a Corona-chugging contest. For Arjun, the trip was a much-needed break from work, and while it had certainly helped him unwind, he hadn't gotten much sleep over the weekend. Every time Arjun and Ali tried to sneak in a nap, Karan barged into their rooms. 'I'm getting married, fuckers. Wake up and let's party!'

The man was out of control.

'You're getting married,' Ali groaned, pulling a pillow over his head. 'You're not *dying*.'

'A married man is as good as a dead man,' Angad said philosophically, taking a long drag of his joint. Angad Vir Singh was known in Columbia University as Angad 'Weed' Singh, and in Ludhiana as Angad Vir Singh Bagga, king of hosiery and textile fabrics. At 5'5" and 120 kg, Angad's opinion held weight, literally. 'Let's party, bro,' Angad said in his characteristic monotone. Ali and Arjun had dragged themselves out of bed, unshaven and bleary-eyed, prepared to do some more damage to their livers.

Arjun stifled a yawn and pressed his fingers to his temples. He had to review a presentation for the upcoming board meeting and then he needed to get some sleep. He couldn't afford to be sleep-deprived and cranky during Chinky's wedding week.

'Mr Khanna,' the over-friendly flight attendant from before stepped in front of him. 'How may I help you?' she asked, throwing back her shoulders and thrusting her chest forward.

'Just two bottles of water, please,' Arjun said briskly.

'Why don't you take a seat, sir? I'll bring them right over,' she suggested, bending over to look for water bottles and giving Arjun an ample view of her ass, tight skirt and all.

Arjun spotted an entire carton of bottled water at eye level. He swiped one and returned to his seat.

A minute later, the flight attendant appeared with two water bottles. She leaned over him and placed them on his retractable table, practically shoving her breasts in his face. Arjun pressed back into his seat and shot her a discouraging look. He was all for harmless flirting but this woman just wasn't his type. Too much make-up, too little personality.

'Thanks,' he said brusquely.

'We'll be starting our service shortly, Mr Khanna. Do let me know if you'd like anything *special*.' She winked.

Even the strippers in Vegas had been subtler.

'Sure,' he responded blandly.

'I'm Kritika,' she said with a flirtatious smile before she walked away, swaying her hips deliberately.

The girl on the seat next to him rolled her eyes at Kritika's retreating figure. Then realizing Arjun had witnessed her reaction, she turned away with an embarrassed smile.

Arjun looked at the girl in surprise.

Her brown hair was tied up in a messy bun, a few loose tendrils framing her face, and her bright hazel eyes were glued to her screen. The blush from her earlier embarrassment clung faintly to her cheeks, offsetting the olive undertones in her flawless skin and highlighting her full lips.

She was absolutely stunning.

His window divider was open and, though he didn't remember rolling it down, it sure was a stroke of luck. Had she been sitting here the whole time? How had he not noticed her before?

Close your mouth, Khanna.

Arjun watched her long fingers dance on the keyboard as she typed away intently. He noticed that she wasn't wearing a ring. Kitschy orange watch, but no ring.

He leaned back in his seat and waited for the in-flight service to begin. Food was a great conversation starter.

Hour 10

Risha didn't want to stare, but she couldn't help it.

Was the man sitting next to her undeniably the most gorgeous man she had ever laid eyes on? Probably.

Were his piercing black eyes deeper than the ocean they were flying over? Most likely.

Did his crisp white shirt stretch across his broad shoulders and muscular chest as his Rolex-adorned wrist cut into his steak? Absolutely.

But that's not why Risha was staring.

She was staring because she really wanted his dessert. She knew she should've gone for the chocolate option instead of the mango cheesecake. She could always ask for an additional dessert—this was business class, after all. But her server was, would you believe it, Bitchika. So even the first dessert had been placed on Risha's table with considerable reluctance.

Risha could always wait to ask Connor if he came by. But what if Connor didn't service business class? Maybe that's why he was so scared of Bitchika. Aside from the fact that she *was* quite scary, she probably had seniority over him, because she looked after the rich people, and Connor was stuck with the poor people like Bunty and Bunty's mother, and Risha. She took a deep breath and pressed the call button.

Bitchika appeared, flashing a saccharine smile. 'How may I help you?'

'Um,' Risha said, gesturing to the table next to hers, 'I want that.'

Rolex Guy choked on his water.

Bitchika's eyes widened, the smile wiped clean from her face. 'Excuse me?'

Risha shrugged innocently. 'I tried some but I didn't like it, so I want that instead.'

Bitchika frowned. 'I don't understand.'

'I ordered the mango cheesecake but I want the chocolate thing instead. What's it called?'

A slow, insincere smile spread across Bitchika's face. 'Dark chocolate torte layered with candied praline and créme brûlée.'

'Yes, exactly. I'll have that.'

'I'm so sorry, love. We're all out.'

Risha's face fell. 'You don't have any left?'

'I just gave the last one to Mr Khanna.'

'Who is Mr Khanna?' Risha demanded, mentally prepared to march down to this Mr Khanna's seat and convince him to exchange his dessert with hers.

And that's when Risha saw the first genuine expression cross Bitchika's face: shock. She opened her mouth to answer but no words came out. She turned to Rolex Guy with a bewildered look.

Risha followed her gaze. Rolex Guy looked oddly pleased as he said, 'That would be me. Arjun Khanna.'

'Hi,' she said to his dessert.

He turned to the flight attendant with a charming smile. 'Kritika, it's the strangest thing, but I actually wanted the mango cheesecake instead of this. So I'm just going to trade with Ms . . . ?'

Risha looked from Arjun to Bitchika and back to Arjun. Oh, he meant her. 'Risha. Hi, I'm Risha. And I really appreciate your sacrifice, Mr Khanna.'

He laughed. 'Arjun.' He picked up his plate and handed it to Risha. 'Thanks again, Kritika. You've been a big help.'

Bitchika shot Risha a haughty look before walking away.

Risha sighed. 'She really does not like me.'

'I'm sure she doesn't,' Arjun muttered.

Risha opened her mouth to ask what he meant by that, but got distracted by the chocolate delicacy in front of her. She put a large spoonful in her mouth and closed her eyes, revelling in the complete and utter bliss that was her dessert. This was totally worth Bitchika's wrath. When she opened her eyes she found Arjun watching her with undisguised amusement.

'You really like chocolate,' he mused.

Risha smiled sheepishly. 'Doesn't everyone? Except you, I mean. Oh, here's your cheesecake.'

'Thanks,' Arjun said, reaching for the dessert he neither liked nor wanted. He took a small bite and followed it up with a large gulp of water, as though swallowing a pill. 'It's great,' he lied. And the lie was totally worth it. Risha had little specks of chocolate on her lips and she looked strangely . . . sated.

Arjun looked away abruptly. Was he seriously getting aroused by watching a woman eat dessert?

Get a grip on yourself, Khanna.

'Why does your tattoo say "desi" in Urdu?' Risha asked him between mouthfuls of chocolate cake.

Arjun blinked.

She narrowed her gaze, pointed to his arm and said slowly, 'You *do* know it says that, right?'

'I know. But how do *you* know?'

'I can read Urdu.'

He seemed impressed. 'How come?'

'I learnt it from my grandfather; he was an Urdu poet.'

'Was?'

'He died three years ago.'

'I'm sorry.'

She shook her head. 'It's okay. He was a hundred years old. Literally.'

'Wow.'

'I know! If I ever get a tattoo, it will say "Punjabi" in Punjabi,' she said excitedly.

'Oh, because people will ask what it says and you'll answer "Punjabi", and then they'll ask what the word means and you'll say "Punjabi"?' he ventured.

'Exactly, infinite loop.'

'So let me guess,' he said, scrunching up his face in mock concentration, 'you're . . . Gujarati?'

Risha laughed and the sound drew Arjun's attention to her chocolate-glazed mouth.

He suddenly had an overwhelming desire to taste chocolate. But not off her plate.

He looked away and tried to focus on his dessert. He took another reluctant bite before asking, 'So why haven't you got the tattoo already?'

'I have zero tolerance for pain.' She wrinkled her nose. 'Why does yours say "desi", anyway?'

He looked a little embarrassed. 'My best friend is Pakistani. We were young and foolish and incredibly drunk one night, so we went out and got matching tattoos.'

'That's kinda sweet. Just kidding, it's totally lame.'

He laughed. 'Yes, it is. But after five drinks, it seemed like a good idea.'

'After five drinks, pretty much anything seems like a good idea.'

Weird, he'd just been thinking that. 'I usually just lie about what it says because most people can't read Urdu.'

'Why "desi"?'

'Because we got sick of being asked if we're Indian or Pakistani, so we just called ourselves "desi".'

'Super lame,' she said, licking the back of her spoon. 'I hope you guys are still friends at least, unlike Deepika and Ranbir?'

'Yes, we are. He's in Pakistani politics, so we don't get to meet too often, but we're pretty close.'

'Oh my god, is your friend Bilawal Bhutto?'

Arjun chuckled. 'Thankfully, no.'

'Where did you manage to find a Pakistani best friend, anyway?' she asked.

'We went to the same college in New York,' he explained. 'How about you? Where did you go to college?'

'Punjab. I'm from Amritsar.'

'Do you live in Amritsar?'

She shook her head. 'Delhi. My parents still live in Amritsar, though. What about you?'

'Delhi. Well, Gurgaon actually,' he said, wiping his mouth with a napkin.

'My condolences.'

He laughed. 'I work in Gurgaon, so I save time commuting.'

'Yes, keep telling yourself that if it makes you feel better about living in Gurgaon,' she teased. 'Where do you work?'

He paused, measuring his words. 'I work for a real estate company.'

'Oh. So was LA a work trip?'

'No. A college friend's bachelor party in Vegas.'

'Bilawal?'

'His name is Ali. And no, Ali is already married. This was another friend, Karan,' he said. 'What took you to LA? Holiday?'

'I wish! I was there for a shoot—'

Risha's response was interrupted by Bitchika's sudden appearance. 'I just wanted to let you know that your seat is no longer smelling like faeces and you can go back to where you came from,' she said, emphasizing the last four words.

This woman was unbelievable. Risha really wanted to learn the skill of making scathing comments while flashing a perfect smile. But at that moment she wanted to kill Bitchika. For making it sound like *Risha* had pooped herself, for interrupting a perfectly pleasant conversation with a perfectly nice guy, and for making her feel like she didn't 'belong' in business class.

Risha gritted her teeth. 'I'm comfortable here, thanks. As you know, my TV is broken so I can't possibly continue sitting in that seat. Also, the kid sitting next to me—'

'Yes, he was quite traumatized by the experience. Imagine sitting next to a seat that smells like excreta,' Bitchika said with a cloying smile, still implying that Risha had soiled herself, not Bunty. And she sure knew a lot of words for poop. If Risha didn't hate her guts, she would've forwarded Bitchika's resume to Kabir. The attrition at *Delhi Today* was at an all-time high and Kabir was perpetually on the lookout for people with decent vocabularies. Bitchika seemed like the type of person who would know fancy French words, and that would make her employable in Kabir's eyes.

Risha stole a glance at Arjun. His black eyes were narrowed to angry slits and she wasn't sure if he was glaring at her or at Bitchika. He probably thought she was a poor nobody with no control over her bowel movements.

'Your TV is working just fine,' Bitchika said firmly.

Risha stood up with a resigned sigh. 'Fine, I'll move. But stop making it sound like I pooped in my seat, when you know Bunty is the one who did it.'

Still smiling, Bitchika lowered her voice to a hiss. 'Your little rendezvous is over. Now go back to 32C.'

Wow, she knows how to pronounce 'rendezvous', Risha thought with reluctant admiration. And her lips hadn't even moved as she spoke that disdainful sentence. Evil though she was, Risha could definitely learn a lot from this woman.

Risha stood up and started gathering her things. Her business class dream was too good to be true.

Hour 11

Arjun was in a dilemma.

This girl was smoking hot, surprisingly candid, and funny as hell. And Arjun had really been enjoying their conversation until she mentioned that she'd visited LA for a 'shoot'.

Was she a model? Because he had a mild aversion to models. He had dated one a while ago and that had *not* ended well. When Risha stood up in response to Kritika's obviously childish ploy, he had looked up at her in surprise. Because she didn't seem like the type to back down from a fight, but also because she was much taller than he had expected.

Her skinny jeans accentuated her long legs and her white top rode up a little as she reached into the overhead bin, giving him a peek of her tiny waist and shapely curves. Arjun liked tall girls because he liked that he could make eye contact with them easily. But tall or short, he did *not* like models. In fact, the only people he disliked more than models were journalists.

With that body and those looks, Risha had to be a model. Except she wasn't wearing any make-up, unless you counted the sticky chocolate that tinted her lips.

Think, Khanna.

What other people went to shoots? Brand managers, advertising executives, production managers, directors, photographers, actors, stylists, set designers, make-up artists.

Arjun frowned. He really didn't want to spend the next nine hours indulging Kritika's attention-seeking theatrics. On the other hand, if Risha was a model, this was a lucky escape. But if she *wasn't* a model . . .

Arjun made a decision.

'Risha, sit down. Kritika and I will be back in a minute.'

Risha frowned at his tone, but did as he asked.

Arjun switched his gaze to the flight attendant. 'Do you mind accompanying me?'

Kritika knew it wasn't a question and she followed him silently. At the galley, Arjun folded his arms and straightened to his full height. 'Is it a norm in this airline to downgrade a passenger who has been upgraded?'

'No, Mr Khanna, but—'

'I want to buy the seat next to mine,' Arjun said in a tone he usually reserved for acquiring a property.

Kritika's jaw dropped. 'Mr Khanna, that won't be necessary.'

Arjun gave her an icy glare. 'I didn't think so.'

She gulped and gave him a nervous nod.

'One more thing,' he said frostily. 'I want you to stop bothering the woman seated next to me. In fact, I want someone else to service our lounge.'

Kritika's eyes widened and she nodded emphatically. From the moment Arjun had stood up in his seat, he knew he would get his way. But just because he couldn't resist putting this nasty woman in her place, he casually added, 'If there's a problem, I can speak to the airline's CEO—he's a friend.'

With a terrified shake of her head, Kritika rasped, 'Yes, sir. Of course. I mean, no! There's no problem, Mr Khanna.'

Arjun returned to his seat without another word.

Risha looked at him expectantly. 'Should I move?'

'No.'

'How come?' she asked.

'I asked her nicely if you could stay.'

She gave him a sceptical look. 'You asked her *nicely*?'

'Something like that,' he said evasively. Then he paused and looked her in the eye. 'Earlier you said that you were returning from a shoot?'

Moment of truth.

'Yes, I was shooting a wedding in LA. I'm a photographer.'

And suddenly, it all came back to him.

Dear Bhai,

Here's the link to the photographer's website. Her name is Risha Kohli and she'll be taking candid photos at the wedding. She's only shot a few weddings but I love her work and she comes highly recommended by Vikram and his wife.

Below that, there was a link to her website, but Arjun hadn't clicked on it. Chinky had been sending him so many wedding-related updates that he barely managed to skim through them. Now he wished he had read that particular email.

'You're Risha Kohli.'

'Yup. Wait, how do you know my last name?'

'You're shooting Nitisha Khanna's wedding next week.'

Risha was shocked. 'How do you know that?'

'She's my sister.'

Her face broke into a wide grin. 'No way!'

'I'm surprised you didn't guess we're related. Khanna is such an uncommon name,' he joked.

'Any relation to Rahul Khanna?'

'He's my cousin.'

Her eyes widened. 'Really?'

'Not really.' He grinned.

'Thank god. Because I would have a hard time breathing around him, let alone taking photos.' She laughed.

'So you're not a model?'

She gave him a puzzled look. 'Uh, no. What gave you that impression?'

Your long legs, your curvy waist and your gorgeous smile.

'You said you were returning from a shoot, so I assumed . . .'

Her eyes danced with amusement. 'That's the first time I've ever been mistaken for a model!'

Arjun found that hard to believe. 'Fishing for compliments?' he asked, wondering if he had inadvertently got himself stuck next to a narcissist.

Risha shook her head. 'No, seriously, to qualify as a model I would need to lose at least twenty kilos and thirty IQ points.'

Arjun burst out laughing. He had made the right decision.

Hour 12

Risha stole a furtive glance at Arjun. For the last half hour, they had been browsing through Nidhi and Vikram's wedding photos in an attempt to find a picture of Arjun. His dark eyes were narrowed in concentration and he scratched his stubble absently as he scrolled through hundreds of photos.

Risha couldn't believe this guy. He was surprisingly normal for someone who was successful, handsome and had a smile *literally* worth a million bucks. Her interaction with 'famous' people had been limited to socialites during her Page 3 days, and most of them were first-rate assholes. But despite his enormous wealth and Ivy League background, Arjun seemed like someone she could easily be friends with.

Or more.

The thought had come from nowhere and she drew in a sharp breath.

Arjun looked up. 'What?'

'Are you sure you were at the wedding?' she asked him for the third time.

'For only thirty minutes, but, yes,' Arjun assured her, running a hand through his unruly black hair.

Unable to find a photo of Arjun in the 'shortlist' folder, Risha had fished out the original dump of two thousand photos. Up till now they had spotted three Bollywood actors, half a dozen politicians and the entire Indian cricket team. But no Arjun.

'Oh, here's a good one of Chinky.'

'Chinky?' Risha asked.

'Nitisha. It's her nickname but she hates it.'

'Nicknames are meant to be hated,' Risha said.

'Do you have a nickname?' he wondered.

'No,' she said, a little too quickly.

'If I guess will you tell me?' he asked.

'No.'

'Bubbly?' he guessed.

'No.'

'Sonu?' he ventured, a glint of amusement in his eyes.

'No.'

'Guddu?' he asked, unable to hide his smile.

'No. And can we get back to the task at hand?' she asked, taking her laptop back from him. 'What time did you arrive at the venue?'

'I don't know. Around eight o'clock, I guess. But it doesn't matter because I'm convinced you didn't take a picture of me,' he said.

'That's impossible,' she muttered, sorting the photos by timestamp.

'I doubt you'll get paid if you don't take pictures of me at Chinky's wedding,' he grinned.

Risha ignored him and kept scrolling.

Arjun watched her in silence and his thoughts went back to the question he had asked her earlier. 'No offence, but why did the LA couple call a photographer all the way from India?'

She had smiled. 'It's a fair question. My cousin and the bride are co-workers. He showed the couple some of my photos and they liked my work. Plus, it was cheaper to fly me from India than to hire a local photographer.'

Arjun had appreciated her honesty. But after looking through Risha's work, he could understand why the LA couple, or even Chinky, had chosen her. Risha's photos were very impressive—artistic without being pompous, beautiful without being overbearing, and filled with bright, warm colours. Her photography, Arjun mused, was a bit like her personality.

A few minutes later, Risha finally found what she was looking for. 'Aha! I knew it had to be here somewhere,' she said, but her triumphant smile quickly turned into a frown.

'What's wrong?' he asked, reading her expression.

'It's a side profile and it's shaky,' she said in a disappointed voice.

Arjun turned the screen to face him. 'Yes, but it *is* me.'

'Only one photo of you and that too blurry,' she said, sounding annoyed.

'Maybe you couldn't keep a steady hand once you laid eyes on this handsome face,' he said, flashing her a white smile.

Risha was not amused. 'How did this happen?'

Even though his tone was flippant, Risha sensed he wasn't joking when he said, 'Because I planned it that way.'

She tipped her head. 'You're camera-shy?'

He paused. 'I wouldn't put it exactly that way, but, yes, I don't like being photographed.'

'That's a pity,' she blurted.

'Why?'

Because it's a crime to deny the world the pleasure of seeing your beautiful face.

'Because I'm a photographer and I think everyone should . . . like being photographed,' she said, hoping he would buy her lame explanation.

'I'm not a fan of public attention,' he said quietly.

'Lucky for you, your job doesn't require you to make any public appearances like, I don't know, inaugurating tall buildings.' She snorted.

He looked at her in surprise. 'You read the interview?'

Oops.

'I glanced at the newspaper when you went to the restroom,' she said casually. And only so she could wipe the smug smile off his face, she added, 'Are you sure you're 6'2"? You look more like 5'11".'

His voice deepened a notch. 'Would you like me to stand up so you can take a good look?'

'No, thanks,' she said dryly. 'But at the wedding, I'll make sure I only shoot you when you're *sitting down*.'

Hour 13

Arjun couldn't believe this girl.

It was obvious she hadn't known who he was at first, but now that she did, she didn't seem intimidated by him in the least. Nor was she throwing herself at him. Meeting a stranger and being able to have a normal conversation with them was uncharted territory for Arjun.

Upon moving back to India, in addition to losing his privacy, Arjun had also lost the ability to make new friends. Even though he worked really hard to stay out of the limelight, people eventually connected the dots and figured out who he was. Sure, he was used to female attention since even before taking over the reins of the Khanna fortune, but at least back in New York, he could date a girl without worrying about their picture showing up in the tabloids.

To be fair, Arjun's face wasn't exactly plastered in the media, but for reasons unbeknown to him, the press had recently developed a keen interest in his personal life. Arjun's life was fairly uneventful and, aside from work-related functions, he avoided public appearances and absolutely steered clear of Delhi's party scene.

The only rationale for the media's curiosity about him was their interest in Rohan and Nitisha's wedding. As the founder and CEO of an e-commerce startup that had recently raised a billion dollars, Rohan was the media's darling. And as the face behind designer label Khudai, Nitisha was an up-and-coming name in the Indian fashion industry. So Arjun guessed that he was famous by association, and hoped that the media frenzy would die down after the wedding. Some people, he thought drolly, had greatness thrust upon them.

But the girl sitting next to him didn't seem thrown off by his wealth or fame. If anything, she was amused by it. She teased him, laughed at him and even—he thought with chagrin—implied that he was *short*. She probably wouldn't care if she found out the threat he had issued to Kritika to keep Risha in her seat. Actually, he intuited, she would probably be more annoyed than flattered by what he had done.

'Why,' Arjun wondered out loud, 'did you agree to move back to economy?'

'Well, technically I haven't paid for this seat. I thought it would be unfair to take advantage of a fortuitous situation.' Risha shrugged.

Was this girl for real?

'You would rather sit in a seat that *literally* smells like crap than fight with a jealous flight attendant?'

'Obviously I wouldn't prefer it, but—wait, what do you mean "jealous"?'

'Don't be obtuse, Risha.'

'Oh, because you're so hot and all the women are in love with you?' She rolled her eyes.

His mouth quirked into a lazy smile. 'You think I'm hot?'

'No, I don't!' she sputtered.

'Way to massage a guy's ego,' he retorted dryly.

Risha mumbled something about having to use the restroom and disappeared. For forty-five minutes.

Hour 14
News Today Office Messenger Chat
Participants: Risha_K, Nidhi13

Risha_K: Guess who's sitting next to me on the flight?

Nidhi13: Narendra Modi?

Risha_K: Sure, because the prime minister of India travels by a private foreign airline.

Nidhi13: It's possible.

Risha_K: Modi is in Tajikistan. It's on the front page of the newspaper you work for! How do you not know this?

Nidhi13: Sorry, I only read Page 3.

Risha_K: I sincerely hope that's a joke. And no, not Modi—he only flies Air India.

Nidhi13: Aishwarya Rai?

Risha_K: I'm flying back from LA, not Cannes.

Nidhi13: Hmmm, is it a Hollywood actor? Is it George Clooney? Please say it's George Clooney!

Risha_K: I wish. It's not someone famous.

Nidhi13: Someone from *NT*? The IT guy who has a crush on you?

Risha_K: An IT guy has a crush on me?

Nidhi13: You think your Internet just stops working on its own? It's a carefully plotted scheme so he can visit your workstation and be your knight in shining armour.

Risha_K: If that's true, I'm going to kill him.

Nidhi13: Don't say incriminating things on office messenger.

Risha_K: It's not the IT guy. It's no one from *NT*. God, you really suck at this.

Nidhi13: At least give me a hint.

Risha_K: He's related to a fashion designer who is currently in the news for something.

Nidhi13: Well, that one fashion designer is in the news for copying the designs of that other fashion designer. Is it one of them?

Risha_K: You are useless. I can't believe I'm standing in the bathroom having this conversation!

Nidhi13: The business class bathroom actually has space to stand? Wow. Okay, since I know you hate texting and generally doing stuff on your phone, I'm going to take my final guess.

Risha_K: . . .

Nidhi13: Rohan Singhal?

Risha_K: Close, but no. I'm sitting next to Nitisha Khanna's brother.

Nidhi13: Arjun Khanna isn't 'not famous'. There's a picture of him on today's business page.

Risha_K: Ha! You *do* read more than just Page 3.

Nidhi13: Actually, we had a bet in the lunchroom on which page has the maximum number of typos, and I said business—which is why I had to read it.

Risha_K: I swiped his newspaper while he was away from his seat.

Nidhi13: Um, ever heard of e-paper? I can't believe you're sitting next to Arjun Khanna—it's the uncanniest thing ever. Do you know he attended my wedding?

Risha_K: I know!

Nidhi13: I just googled him and he's hot! Although there are hardly any pictures of him online—just a couple of them repeated in different sizes and resolutions. But he's really good-looking. You better walk out of that plane bearing either his ring or his child. Don't let me down.

Risha_K: Are you crazy? He probably has a super-hot girlfriend in every city in the world.

Nidhi13: Oh, I see. So that's the only thing keeping you from procreating with him?

Risha_K: Pretty much. He's ridiculously hot, super funny, and he hasn't even tried to look down my shirt. The only thing wrong with him is that he doesn't like chocolate. Aside from that, he's quite perfect.

Nidhi13: Someone has a little crush on their client's brother. Way to keep it professional, Rish.

Risha_K: It's not like I'm going to *do* anything about it. He's like a zillionaire, he can probably buy the business class lounge.

Nidhi13: Actually, he can probably buy the entire airline. But why does that matter?

Risha_K: It doesn't matter to *me*.

Nidhi13: You'd be surprised by the number of rich people that don't care about money.

Risha_K: Because they can 'afford' not to. Get it?

Nidhi13: Funny. Oooh, just found a photo of him smiling. He looks a bit like Fawad Khan.

Risha_K: As if! The only person that looks like Fawad Khan *is* Fawad Khan. OHMYGOD! I just saw my reflection in the mirror and I look like crap. I have chocolate all over my face, my hair looks like a bird's nest, and my face looks generally hideous. I cannot believe I spent the last four hours looking like this. No wonder he hasn't been flirting with me. Am I really so unflirtable?

Nidhi13: 'Unflirtable' is not a word. I can't believe you're an assistant editor. Also, you're incapable of looking hideous. I personally know at least three people at *NT* who are in love with you.

Risha_K: Kabir, the IT guy and . . . who's the third?

Nidhi13: Charan.

Risha_K: Who the hell is Charan?

Nidhi13: The marketing intern.

Risha_K: Whatever.

Nidhi13: I'm serious. He goes into a wide-eyed coma every time he sees you, and he told one of the editorial interns that you are 'marriage material'. And as you know, what happens in the editorial department never stays in the editorial department.

Risha_K: I'm flattered. My list of admirers includes my snobby boss, some lame IT guy and a hormonal teenager.

Nidhi13: And maybe Arjun Khanna. Why don't you brush your hair, wear some make-up and turn that 'maybe' into 'definitely'?

Risha_K: I might have some mascara in my bag.

Nidhi13: Negative. It's a long flight; if you fall asleep and it smudges, you might end up with raccoon eyes. Better no make-up than bad make-up.

Risha_K: This is fourteen-hour-lasting waterproof mascara. I wore it to your wedding.

Nidhi13: Am I the only person who didn't cry at my wedding?

Risha_K: Yup. Introducing the most insensitive bride since Julia Roberts in *Runaway Bride*— Nidhi Marwah.

Nidhi13: Can you please Photoshop some tears on to the wedding photos?

Risha_K: I'm opposed to Photoshopping.

Nidhi13: What about airbrushing?

Risha_K: Yuck.

Nidhi13: So, basically anything that enables people to improve their physical appearance?

Risha_K: No, LASIK is okay.

Nidhi13: What a relief. Send me a picture once you're done getting all gussied up for your new lover.

Risha_K: mascara.jpg

Nidhi13: Only in one eye?

Risha_K: Crap, seems like I ran out. Perfect timing. Now I'll be walking around with one eye looking nicer than the other.

Nidhi13: Just wipe it off.

Risha_K: I can't! My make-up remover is in my check-in luggage.

Nidhi13: Try water.

Risha_K: This mascara is invincible. An hour of sobbing at your wedding didn't smudge it, but *water* will? Thanks, Nidhi.

Nidhi13: He's a boy, he probably won't even notice the length of your eyelashes.

Risha_K: Well, at least I did the eye that's closer to him. Maybe I'll wear an eye patch on the other eye.

Nidhi13: Oooh, yes. Send me a picture.

Risha_K: That was a joke.

Nidhi13: Oh. I mean LOL.

Risha_K: :-(

Nidhi13: Relax! You only have a few more hours to go, try to get some sleep. Maybe you can wear one of those eye masks they give you on the plane, that way he won't be able to see your eyes at all.

Risha_K: Sleeping is a good idea. I land at three in the morning and I have to be at work by nine.

Nidhi13: Vikram and I will pick you up from the airport.

Risha_K: Thanks, but Rishabh already said he's picking me up.

Nidhi13: I know I've said this eighteen thousand times before, but it's really strange that you still hang out with your ex-boyfriend. Even if he is gay.

Risha_K: We only dated for a month in school, it doesn't count. Plus, he's one of my best friends.

Nidhi13: *I'm* your best friend.

Risha_K: Only if you show up at all the Khanna–
Singhal wedding functions.

Nidhi13: I kinda have to because of the bromance
between the groom and my husband.

Risha_K: Have you spent a lot of time with Nitisha
and Rohan?

Nidhi13: We do dinner with them once a month;
more often when Vikram isn't travelling.

Risha_K: I didn't get to spend much time with them
at your wedding.

Nidhi13: Don't worry, they're super nice.

Risha_K: Cheesy pre-wedding shoots are a great way
to break the ice, but since they had no time
before, I'm meeting them directly at the
first event.

Nidhi13: I'm sure you guys will hit it off; they're both
pretty cool. Rohan is a little on the quieter
side, but Nitisha is very friendly.

Risha_K: Yes, she sounds quite friendly in her emails,
and her sibling is fun to talk to. Hopefully
they are a normal family.

Nidhi13: Future in-laws, you mean.

Risha_K: Hilarious.

Nidhi13: Jokes apart, Rohan is pretty important to
Vikram, and vice versa. You know Rohan
picked the wedding date to accommodate
Vikram's cricket schedule?

Risha_K: Wow, I didn't realize they're that close.

Nidhi13: And they only spent a year together at the
Mumbai Cricket Academy when they were
teenagers.

Risha_K: No way! Rohan wanted to play cricket
professionally?

Nidhi13: Yes, but luckily for Nitisha, he moved back to Delhi before the 'Mumbai is better than Delhi' bug bit him. Grrr.

Risha_K: Vikram STILL says that?

Nidhi13: Vikram has conveniently forgotten that he spent the best years of his life in Delhi before moving to Mumbai.

Risha_K: Yes, I've heard Mumbai does that to people.

Nidhi13: But since he finally chose to settle down in Delhi, I think he secretly loves Delhi more than Mumbai.

Risha_K: Uh, I think the reason he settled down in Delhi is that he loves *you* more than Mumbai.

Nidhi13: That too :-)

Risha_K: Your husband has magazine covers dedicated to his good looks, hair that belongs in a shampoo commercial, and let's not forget those killer abs. All he needs to do is lose that ridiculous Bambaiya vocab, and he would be perfect.

Nidhi13: The last time we were in Lajpat Nagar market for chaat, the golgappa wala refused to serve Vikram because he kept calling it 'pani puri'.

Risha_K: Seriously?

Nidhi13: Well, he refused to serve Vikram because one of the newspapers that morning had called Vikram a 'Mumbai boy' and the golgappa wala wanted Vikram to veto that claim and admit he's *actually* a Delhi boy.

Risha_K: Did he?

Nidhi13: No, but he said some cheesy line about Delhi being his sasural, and by virtue of that the golgappa wala practically being his in-law.

Risha_K: Awww.

Nidhi13: That was the golgappa wala's reaction too. But after we left the chaat place, Vikram turns to me and whispers, 'The pani puri place in Bandra is so much better.'

Risha_K: He did not!

Nidhi13: Oh, that's not all. He even said he prefers the kathi rolls at Bade Miya to Khan Chacha.

Risha_K: He is SO dead.

Nidhi13: According to him, Big Chill is Delhi's *only* saving grace.

Risha_K: How are you married to such a freak?

Nidhi13: I ask myself the same question every day. Better find out Arjun Khanna's stand on Delhi vs Mumbai before you get too serious.

Risha_K: Just so you know, I'm rolling my eyes.

Nidhi13: Both of them or just the one with mascara?

Risha_K: Ha ha. I'm heading back to my seat now.

Nidhi13: See you at work tomorrow. Have a safe flight!

Hour 15

By the time Risha made her way back to her seat, Arjun was asleep. His legs were propped up on his footrest and though his seat wasn't reclined all the way, he looked comfortable. Like he was used to sleeping in awkward positions.

For the first time since she had met him, Risha allowed herself the treat of feasting her eyes on Arjun.

Her gaze travelled from the errant black lock that grazed his brow to the dark lashes that rested on his cheeks. He had a sharp, aristocratic nose and his square jaw was clenched tight, as though his dreams plagued him. Strangely, he had seemed more relaxed awake than asleep, and Risha couldn't help but wonder what he was dreaming about. His hard chest moved in tandem with his deep breaths and his hands were locked neatly at his stomach. His blanket had slid halfway to the floor, and Risha stood up and draped it over his legs. Then she reached up and turned off his overhead light. The faint cabin light streamed across his handsome features, and she had an inexplicable urge to reach out and touch his unshaven face.

And it was in that precise moment that Risha knew she was in trouble.

Because instead of worrying about her unmascaraed eye, she was suddenly very concerned about spending the next few days in close proximity with this man.

Way to keep it professional, Rish.

Hour 17

'Mr Khanna.' A voice brought him to consciousness.

Arjun's head hurt, either from too little sleep or too much. Too little, he guessed, because he couldn't remember the last time he had slept too much.

He opened his eyes reluctantly and saw a male flight attendant hovering over him. The cabin lights had been switched back on and he could hear the distant murmur of the crew in the background.

'Sir, we are about to land. For your safety, I request you to fasten your seat belt and bring your seat back to a full upright pos—'

'Yes, thanks.' Arjun knew the drill.

The flight attendant gave Risha an appreciative look before walking away.

Arjun sat up in his seat and glanced at Risha. She gave him a sleepy smile. 'Good morning.'

'Hey,' he said groggily. 'Did you get any sleep?'

'Not much,' she said.

'Do you have to work tomorrow?'

'Yes, but I can sleep in.'

Arjun nodded, then stared out the window in silence. He was a morning person, in the sense that he woke up at 5 a.m. every day and ran ten kilometres, but he wasn't particularly talkative this time of day. He was a little relieved that Risha didn't try to initiate conversation because he didn't want to come across as grumpy.

Hour 18

By the time they finished immigration and arrived at the baggage carousel, Arjun was fully awake. Which is why he didn't fall over in shock when a little boy poked him in the stomach. 'Oye, so you are her boyfriend?'

With her hands on her hips, Risha gave the boy an admonishing look. 'Bunty, that's enough.'

A lady, who Arjun presumed was Bunty's mother, strolled her luggage cart towards them, screeching at her son, 'Bunty, *tu Amritsar toh chal*! I will tell to your daddy what you are doing to strangers.'

Bunty's hands flew to his crotch and he shifted uncomfortably. 'Mummy, I want to toilet.'

Bunty's mother threw Arjun an apologetic look. 'Raylee sorry, bhai saab. He is very naughty boy.'

Arjun was flummoxed. 'Uh, it's all right.'

She started after Bunty in the direction of the restrooms, wheeling her trolley like a race cart. Hoping for an explanation, Arjun turned to Risha, but she was running to catch up with Bunty's mother. From a distance, he saw Risha fish something out of her purse and hand it to Bunty's mother. The lady broke into a wide-toothed grin and gathered Risha in a hug. Risha hugged her back warmly before walking back to a puzzled Arjun.

'What was that?' Arjun asked, catching the satisfied smile on her face.

'That's the little boy I was sitting next to in economy. I have a feeling he has irritable bowel syndrome, what with him visiting the bathroom so frequently. I think it gets triggered by anxiety,' she said, speaking more to herself than to Arjun.

'What did you give to his mother?'

'Oh, that. I gave her my dad's card—he's a gastroenterologist in Amritsar—she can take Bunty to his clinic,' Risha explained.

Arjun stared at her.

'What?' she asked.

'That was a nice thing to do.'

Risha waved her hand dismissively. 'It's no big deal. I felt bad for the kid.'

'You just carry around your dad's visiting card?'

'*Cards*,' she said wryly. 'My parents are a little paranoid about me living alone in Delhi, so carrying Papa's card is on the list of things I had to agree to before they let me move here.'

'What else is on the list?' he asked, warm amusement filling his eyes.

She started counting on her fingers. 'No public transportation after 8 p.m., no watching late-night movies, no boys in the house, no drinking and driving, no—'

'How many of these rules do you actually follow?'

'All of them,' she said, like that was the most obvious thing.

Arjun gave her an incredulous look.

She shrugged. 'There was no other way they would let their only child move to the big bad city all by herself. It's a small price to pay.' Then she pointed to something. 'Oh, there's my suitcase!'

Arjun grimaced at the pink Samsonite suitcase that crawled its way to them on the conveyor belt. 'I'll get it.'

'No, I can manage,' Risha said, taking a step forward.

Arjun had no doubt that she could, but he'd be damned if he let a woman pick up luggage in his presence. 'No,' he said firmly. 'I will.'

'Thank you,' Risha said politely. She wasn't one of those women who had a point to prove by picking up suitcases or opening her own doors or whatever. So she decided to indulge in this rare display of male chivalry. Arjun lifted the suitcase like it weighed nothing and placed it on her luggage cart.

As they strolled towards the exit, he asked, 'Since it's past 8 p.m., can I give you a ride home?'

'Thanks, but I have a friend picking me up.'

Arjun frowned. 'Delhi is unsafe at this hour, especially for two girls.'

She bit back a smile, imagining how Rishabh would react to being called a 'girl'. He would surely throw a mini tantrum. 'Yes, but it's safe for a girl and a *guy*, which my friend is. In fact, we can give you a ride if you want.'

Arjun stiffened a little. 'No, that's okay. My car is parked in the lot.'

'You left it here the entire weekend?'

Five days, actually. 'Yes.'

'Spoilt rich kid,' she teased.

'It was nice meeting you, Ms Kohli,' Arjun said, holding out his hand.

'Likewise, Mr Khanna,' she replied, mimicking his formal tone. She was about to take his hand, but her phone rang and she answered it without looking. 'Are you here? Okay, same spot. See you in a minute.' She hung up and started reaching out her hand, but Arjun had already withdrawn his.

Risha felt an irrational stab of disappointment. She wanted to shake his hand.

Only because it was the polite thing to do—not because she wanted an excuse to touch him or anything.

'Guess I'll see you around,' he said, staring into her eyes.

Why was he looking at her like that? 'Yes, on Thursday.'

'Thursday?'

'Nitisha's mehndi.'

'Yes, of course. See you on Thursday.'

Risha saw Arjun walk away in the opposite direction, and she exhaled. She hadn't realized she was holding her breath.

Hour 19

Arjun turned off the music in his car. He needed silence to process the events of the last few hours. He was surprised, and a little unsettled, by how Risha and he had just . . .

clicked. Since moving back to India, Arjun had spent too much time around 'perfect' girls. Perfectly painted nails, perfectly painted face and a perfectly painted smile. The vapid conversation starters had left him jaded with the dating scene. 'Real estate is really booming in NCR, isn't it?' or 'Can you guess what brand I'm wearing? Khudai!' or the more direct ones, 'I'm up for a night of fun, no strings attached.' Just thinking about them made him nauseated.

Risha, on the other hand, seemed real. For one thing, she had no idea just how beautiful she was. In the short walk from the luggage carousel to the exit, she had turned a dozen male heads without the slightest clue to their admiring glances.

She was beautiful with those big brown eyes, smooth skin, and hair piled artlessly atop her head. And, he thought with a grin, those chocolate-coated lips. Obviously he was attracted to her, but he also liked the fact that she was talented, independent and *nice*. How many girls did he know that he could call 'nice'?

Arjun was amazed by how drawn he was to her. And a little annoyed, because right before Risha had answered her phone, he had glanced at the caller's name on the screen: Rishabh ICE. Arjun knew ICE meant 'in case of emergency'. If this guy was her emergency contact, they had to be more than just friends. Who the hell was Rishabh and why hadn't Risha mentioned him? She had no business flirting with Arjun if she had a goddamn boyfriend.

Although, he thought with a twinge of disappointment as he pulled into his parking spot in Khanna Heights, she hadn't been flirting with him. Sure, she'd been friendly throughout the flight, but maybe that's all it was, a pleasant conversation with a stranger on a plane. It was also likely that she was being nice because he was the brother of a client.

Arjun remembered Risha's response when he'd asked her if she found him hot. She had denied it with such fervour that Arjun was almost offended. But now he attributed her reaction to this Rishabh guy. She could've at least mentioned the asshole was her boyfriend, instead of calling him a 'friend'.

What the hell is the matter with you, Khanna? You just met the girl. And how transparent was the 'Delhi is unsafe for two girls' comment?

With a sigh, Arjun turned off the ignition and grabbed his suitcase. Striding into the elevator, he whipped out his phone to catch up on email.

'Who was the hottie you were standing with, Kohli?' Rishabh demanded.

Risha rolled her eyes. 'Hello to you too, Rishabh. I'm doing fine, how about yourself?'

'I'm great! I've been told the Ranveer Singh moustache really suits me.'

She gave him an 'oh, please' look. 'If Ranveer Singh found out, the first thing he would do is reach for his razor.'

He gave her a wicked grin. 'Oh, I'd let him shave me any time he wants.'

'Ewww!' she cried.

'Don't be such a vestal virgin, Kohli. Now spit it out, who was the hottie?'

So much for avoiding the topic. 'Um, just this guy who was sitting next to me on the plane. We just, um, walked out together,' she said evasively.

'Let's hope he at least walked out with your number.'

'Please! Like I would ever give my number to a guy I just met.' She snorted.

'This is why you haven't gotten laid in the last, oh, I don't know, *ever*! I'm all about giving my number to guys I just met—a little meaningless sex is good for health.'

'I don't believe in—'

'Meaningless sex, yes, I know. Or plastic surgery, or pizza. Basically anything that's good for your health.'

Her jaw dropped. 'Plastic surgery? Please tell me you're not considering it.'

He shrugged. 'It's an occupational hazard, babe. All the other models are doing it, I can't be the only one without ass implants.'

'Your ass is just fine, Rishabh. Now get this ridiculous plastic surgery idea out of your head, or I'll call your parents and tell on you.'

'Fine, then I'll call your parents and tell them you broke the cardinal "no boys in the apartment" rule.'

She cocked her head. 'Who are you talking about?'

'Me.'

Risha laughed. 'You don't count.'

He shot her a look.

'Because they trust you,' she added quickly.

'Or because they know I prefer dicks to chicks,' he said dryly.

'Well, that too,' she confessed.

'While I'm enjoying your attempts at circumvention, you've never been good at keeping secrets, Kohli. Now tell me about the hot guy, before we reach your building and I have to get into another session with my nemesis.'

Rishabh's 'nemesis' was Tyagiji, the barrel-chested Haryanvi security guard at Risha's building. Thanks to her mother's *besan* laddoos and her father's generous tips each time they visited, Tyagiji watched over Risha like a beefeater guarding the queen. Aside from grunting at Rishabh once when he had reversed his car too close to a pillar, and sneering at him another time when he showed up wearing women's clothing for a costume party, Tyagiji refused to acknowledge his existence. Rishabh was constantly trying out new ways to befriend Tyagiji, but so far he had not succeeded in breaking the guard's steely resolve.

Risha responded to Rishabh's question. 'Arjun Khanna.'

'The name sounds familiar.'

'He was on the *NT* business page today.'

Rishabh gagged. 'Like I would *ever* read the business page. I only read Page 3.'

'Why do people keep saying that? You *do* know I'm no longer on the Page 3 beat?'

'No wonder their quality has gone up.'

'Thanks,' she said dryly.

'It's true. Although, I really loved your last article on healthy food.'

'It was good, right?' Risha beamed.

'Absolutely,' he assured her, even though he had no clue. All he knew was that Risha wrote about health and lifestyle, and most of her articles were either about healthy eating or fitness. Since the odds were fifty-fifty, he'd gone with food. 'Arjun Khanna. I've definitely heard that name before.'

'He's the CEO of Khanna Developers.'

'Nope, doesn't ring a bell.'

'He's Nitisha Khanna's brother,' she said, dreading the turn she knew the conversation would take at the mention of Nitisha.

'I might've read about him in the society pages.'

Having recently learnt about Arjun's aversion to society events, Risha doubted it. But because she wanted to change the topic from Nitisha and her brother, she nodded and opened her mouth to comment on the weather. 'Delhi is really—'

'So he's hot *and* rich. No wonder you didn't give him your number.'

Only because he didn't ask.

Risha frowned at the direction of her thoughts. Arjun was a virtual stranger, and had he asked, she would've given him a fake number.

Right?

'Earth to Risha!'

'Sorry, I'm a little tired. What did you say?'

'Did you check with Nitisha if I can be your plus-one to the wedding?'

'For the tenth time, I'm working. There's no way I can bring a plus-one. And as for your ambition of "becoming the face of Khudai for men", I told you I'll speak to her once she returns from the honeymoon. Give it a rest, Rishabh.'

'Fine.' He sulked.

Risha sighed, then remembered something that would definitely get a reaction from him.

'Arjun Khanna thought I was a model!' She smirked.

His expression deadpan, Rishabh said, 'Oh, now I understand why you were walking him out. The poor guy is blind.'

'Just like you were blind when you asked me to our school's farewell dance?' she countered.

'I only asked you because my mother had started suspecting the reason for my collection of shirtless Salman Khan photos was not my interest in bodybuilding,' he said dryly. 'Also, you were the only girl in DPS Amritsar who didn't wear her hair in two braids.'

'That's because I had a "boy cut" until I was eighteen—my mom's version of the male repellent. It sure worked, because the only boy I dated in school turned out to be gay.'

'I was on the fence, but the hair helped me decide,' he teased. 'It's true, Kohli. You turned me gay!'

Risha flicked his ear playfully. It was good to be back home.

PART TWO
THE WEDDING

Five days to the wedding

Amrita Khanna placed her Birkin bag in the crook of her arm and gave her reflection a satisfied nod. She turned to her husband and pouted dramatically. 'How do I look?'

'Lovely,' he grunted, without looking up from his putt.

'Arvind, please! This is the most important event in the wedding.'

Arvind reluctantly drew his attention away from his indoor golf range and gave her a sardonic smile. 'Not the actual ceremony itself?'

She waved away his comment. 'Oho, you know what I mean.'

'Yes, the circus is fairly important,' he muttered.

'Stop calling it that!' Amrita complained. 'It's a *satsang*.'

Arvind gave her a thorough once-over, from the blonde streaks in her chin-length hair, her bright red lips, her animal-print kaftan, down to her unnecessarily high heels. 'You look more appropriately attired for a kitty party than a satsang.'

Amrita looked pleased with his assessment. That's exactly what she'd been aiming for. 'Aside from Priye Ma's Harmony Hex pooja, there's another reason today's satsang is important.'

The instant the question flew out of his mouth, Arvind regretted it. 'What in the world is a "harmony hex"?'

Amrita seemed surprised by his unprecedented interest. 'The Harmony Hexagon,' she explained with gusto, 'represents the six key pillars of a harmonious marriage: faith, understanding, compassion, insight, trust and honesty. I've created an acronym to remember all the pillars: FUCITH.'

Arvind fought to keep a straight face. 'Sounds fitting.'

'Anyway,' she continued, 'the other reason today is very important is because Priye Ma's niece, Divya, is coming to the satsang and she is just puh-fect!'

Arvind frowned for two reasons. First, the more Amrita associated with Priye Ma and her cronies, the more pronounced her south Delhi accent became. And second, he knew exactly where this conversation was going. Eager to return to his golf game, he pre-empted her thoughts. 'For Arjun.'

'Yes!'

'No.'

'What do you mean, dahling?'

'You know *exactly* what I mean. Leave Arjun alone,' he said firmly.

'But, Arvind, I've met her before and she—'

'Have you forgotten the last time you tried to interfere in our son's life?' Arvind said, his voice going up an octave.

Amrita flushed. 'How was I supposed to know that Karishma would turn out to be a slimy little gold-digger?'

Arvind took a deep breath. 'She was a model in the early stages of her career. How did you *not* know?' he said sarcastically. 'I don't stop you from this Science of Living mumbo jumbo because it keeps you occupied. So raise funds, visit yoga camps, do whatever, but I'm not going to stand for this matchmaking rubbish. Arjun is an adult and we have no right to interfere in his life.'

Amrita raised her chin adamantly. 'But all his friends are getting married! First that Pakistani boy, then Karan, I'm sure even that *motu* Angad will find someone. But all Arjun does is work, work and more work. And it doesn't help that he's turning thirty next year—he won't be able to find anyone on his own!'

'That's what you said about Chinky.'

Amrita cringed at the commonplace nickname. 'Nitisha,' she corrected. 'And look who she's found—he's a baniya and, on top of that, he lives in *Rajouri Garden*,' she said with an exaggerated shudder.

'*Rajouri Garden*,' Arvind reminded her scornfully, 'is less than a kilometre from where our first home was—the home in which your son was born. What a convenient memory you have, Amrita.'

Forced to recall a time in her life she had all but erased from her mind, his wife turned bright red. Arvind softened his tone. 'Rohan is completely self-made and I have nothing but respect for him. He is grounded, well brought up, and frankly, I doubt we could've found a better match for Chinky had we tried. We are lucky he's marrying into our family and you would do well to remember that.'

Arvind turned back to his putt and adjusted his stance for his next shot. Realizing the conversation was over, Amrita pushed her shoulders back and strutted out the door, only pausing briefly to issue a reminder. 'Don't be late for the satsang.'

Risha glanced at her watch. She had to finish two more three-hundred-word articles before she called it a day, and it was already 6 p.m. Her desk phone rang and she answered it. 'Hello?'

The security guard from the reception was at the other end. *'Madam, aapke liye courier aaya hai.'*

'Amritsar se?' She sighed.

'Yes, madam.'

Risha headed to the reception, grumbling to herself. It was almost as though her parents were waiting for the busiest time of the day to 'surprise' her with more matrimonial ads. Risha ripped open the envelope as she walked back to her workstation.

News Today courier log
Sender's name: Dr A.K. Kohli, Amritsar
Receiver's name: Risha Kohli, New Delhi
Date of receipt: Feb 23, 2016
Time stamp: 5:59 PM

Smart, handsome, Punjabi Khatri boy belonging to English-speaking family from Delhi seeks bride. Highly qualified: CA, CS, LLB; 33 years, 5'1". Looking for cultured girl from educated family. Caste no bar, age no bar, height no bar. Send biodata to: ca_shankz8@yahoo.co.in

Well-to-do Punjabi baniya business family based in Pathankot owning BMW, Audi, Jaguar (booked, delivery expected by Dec 2016) seeks bride for son (23, 5'11" BA pass correspondence). Girl should be a good mix of modern and traditional, fair complexion must. Call: 0988889933

Risha was spared reading the third ad because she ran into Kabir.

'Just the person I wanted to see,' he said with a smile.

Just the person I didn't, she thought, remembering the pile of work at her desk.

Kabir glanced at the newspaper cuttings in her hand. 'What are you reading?'

Risha pressed the papers to her chest. 'Oh, nothing. Just some research for the "5 Breakfast Smoothies" piece.'

'How's it coming along?' Kabir asked, leaning in a little.

'I'll email it to you before I leave tonight.'

'No rush, you can do it tomorrow,' he said, looking happier than usual.

'Really?'

'Of course. I'm sure you'll do a great job.' He winked.

Wow, he was being friendly.

'Are you drunk?' Risha blurted before she could stop herself.

Kabir chucked her under the chin. 'Three glasses of wine do not a drunk make, cherie.'

'Um, sure,' she said, taking a step back.

'I was at a wine and cheese event,' he explained.

'Which one?'

'The SoL satsang.'

Priye Ma had developed quite a cult following among Delhi's elite. Kabir included apparently, Risha thought with a snort.

Kabir peered at her and Risha faked a cough. His expression turned cold and his tone became patronizing. 'When Delhi's soigné celebrities invite you to a party where each guest receives a personalized Burberry pocket square, you don't just abscond.'

Actually, given the 'no accepting gifts in exchange for news coverage' policy, you do abscond.

Risha arranged her expression into one of polite curiosity. 'How did it go?'

'Fine,' Kabir said nonchalantly. 'They were serving a 1990 Chateau Margaux, so that was nice.'

Risha knew nothing about wine, but she feigned an impressed look. Kabir seldom praised anything, so if he thought the wine was 'nice', Risha was certain it must have been spectacular. 'Sounds like fun. Anyway, I should get back to work.'

Kabir placed a hand on her arm. 'I told you, you can send the article tomorrow.'

And what about the other one I need to write, jackass?

Risha flipped her hair back, casually brushing Kabir's hand away. 'Right, but I think I should get a head start on the other piece: 7 Quick Full-Body Workouts.' And thinking this was the perfect time to slip in the reminder, she added, 'As you know, I'm on leave from Thursday to Sunday.'

'Yes, I remember.' Then he paused, as if considering his next words. 'Do you want to get a drink?'

Risha stared at him. 'Now?'

'Sure.'

Not when she had six hundred words to write. Actually, not ever. Because he was her boss, and while it wasn't exactly frowned upon in their line of work, that wasn't the kind of girl Risha was. 'Uh, we could, but I have to, um . . .' Risha racked her brain for a plausible excuse, 'fix the . . .' Kabir looked at her sceptically and Risha was suddenly struck by a brainwave. 'I have to fix the intern's piece. It was inundated with errors, grammatical and structural, so I offered to help her out.'

It was almost like that one sentence doused Kabir's high. 'I can't believe these people went to *any* school, let alone journalism school. They are the most incompetent, inadequate, ineffectual, unintelligent . . .' and on went the invective.

By the time Risha returned to her workstation, she was exhausted. She had been at work since nine in the morning, working on her articles for the coming week in advance. Earlier today, she had received an email from Nitisha Khanna's wedding planner, Tanvi, containing the week's itinerary.

Risha opened the email again and rolled her eyes at its formal tone. Tanvi was Nidhi's college friend and her wedding planner, and she had worked closely with Risha on two weddings. The girls were good friends, but just like Risha, Tanvi was a thorough professional, so the official-sounding email hardly came as a surprise.

From: Tanvi Bedi <tanvi@irisweddingplanners.in>
To: Risha Kohli <risha.kohli@newstoday.in>
Subject: Khanna–Singhal Wedding Itinerary

Dear Risha,

We look forward to your presence at the wedding festivities of Nitisha and Rohan. For your convenience, please find below the schedule of events. A detailed itinerary with directions and relevant phone numbers is attached with this mail.

February 25 (Thursday)
Mehndi at the Mezzanine Garden, Khanna Heights
The event will commence at 3 p.m. and conclude around 8 p.m.

February 26 (Friday)
Game Night at the Penthouse, Khanna Heights
The event will commence at 8 p.m. and the theme is retro video games.

February 27 (Saturday)
(a) **Cricket Match** at Singhal Farms, Gurgaon
The event will commence at 11 a.m. and conclude after each side has batted twenty overs.
(b) **Cocktails and Dinner** at the Oberoi, Gurgaon
The event will commence at 7.30 p.m. and conclude around midnight.

February 28 (Sunday)
(a) **Choora** at the Bridal Suite of the Oberoi, Gurgaon

The event will take place between 9 a.m. and 10 a.m.
(b) **Bridal Make-up** at the Bridal Suite of the Oberoi, Gurgaon
The event will commence after the choora and is expected to wrap up in two hours.
(c) **Wedding** at the Oberoi, Gurgaon
The ceremony is scheduled for 2 p.m.

Your presence is mandatory at all the above-mentioned events.
A room has been booked in your name at the Oberoi from Feb 27 until the morning of Feb 29. In case you require accommodation prior to that, please let me know.

As per your request, I have scheduled a call with Nitisha at noon tomorrow.

In case you have any questions, please do not hesitate to contact me.

Best,
Tanvi Bedi
Iris Wedding Planners

Risha felt a flutter of excitement in her stomach. Just thinking about the upcoming wedding made the day's exhaustion melt away. Why was it that days without sleep during a shoot didn't make her ornery, but returning to *NT* after a week turned her into a complete grouch? Photography made her so happy that she was actually looking forward to the early mornings and late nights.

And Arjun.

Risha sat up straight in her chair. Maybe lack of sleep wasn't the only reason she was so distracted today, she admitted to herself reluctantly. Maybe she should also account for the unreasonable amount of time she had spent stalking Arjun Khanna on the Internet. She had read every single piece of information she could find on him online. While there weren't too many personal details, there was a lot of material on his accomplishments during his stint as CEO of Khanna Developers.

Absurd as it was, Risha was almost *proud* of him. Like she would be of Nidhi or Rishabh. It was as though she knew Arjun, that she could take pride in his achievements. But she didn't, really. She had just spent a few hours with a guy on a flight. A guy who was intelligent and funny and chivalrous. And really hot.

A guy who had probably forgotten all about her.

Risha could not have been more wrong.

Arjun hadn't forgotten about her. But unlike her, his thoughts were not so pleasantly inclined. To put it mildly, he was livid.

Since getting home that evening, Arjun had spent a significant amount of time googling Risha Kohli. The first result was a LinkedIn profile of some journalist who worked at *News Today*, so Arjun had ignored it. But the other two links were also dead ends; one was a student at the University of Virginia and the other was a human rights lawyer in London. So Arjun had opened the first link again and stared at the profile picture. It was grainy, but that smile was unmistakable.

He read through her profile and found that she had gone to DPS Amritsar and Panjab University before joining *News Today*. Arjun's initial shock had almost instantly turned into anger. He wasn't upset that she had lied to him, but lying about being a *journalist* was another thing altogether. And a goddamn journalist at *News Today*, the country's leading proponent of sensationalized news, inaccurate information and misspelt words.

She had lied to him.

Arjun whipped out his phone and speed-dialled his sister. Nitisha answered in her usual cheerful voice. 'You will live a thousand years! Rohan and I are on our way up to see you.'

'I don't think Risha Kohli is a good choice.'

'Bhai, it's too late now! I've already paid her an advance.'

No wonder Risha hadn't risen to his jibe about not getting paid if she failed to take his photos.

'Wait till you hear the next bit: she's a journalist. A *journalist*, Chinky!' Arjun said.

Last night, he had been crabby about Risha's lack of interest in him, but now he was furious at himself for his naiveté. She had charmed him like a snake.

Nitisha was unfazed. 'I know. She works for *News Today*. Now open the door.'

'You *know*? And you're still letting her shoot your wedding?' Arjun opened the door, still yelling into the phone.

Rohan put his hands up and rocked back on his heels. 'Hello, Arjun. Sorry about Nitisha, she's on the phone with a raving lunatic.'

'Sorry,' Arjun grumbled, shaking Rohan's hand and inviting him in.

Nitisha threw her arms around her brother. 'You have no idea how much I've missed you, Bhai.'

Arjun gave her a concerned look. 'All okay? Mom giving you trouble?'

Nitisha seemed amused. 'No more than she'll be giving *you*.'

'Meaning?'

Nitisha plonked herself on the large sectional sofa in the living room and put her feet up on the wooden coffee table. 'You didn't show up at the SoL satsang today.'

'So? I never attend those things.' Arjun shrugged.

'Yes, but she was hoping to introduce you to someone,' Nitisha explained.

Again, nothing new. This wasn't the first time their mother had attempted something like that, and Arjun knew it wouldn't be the last. But he was impatient to return to the original topic of discussion, so he ignored Nitisha's comment. 'How can you trust a journalist?'

Nitisha grabbed a bowl of walnuts from the table and shrugged. 'She shot Vikram's wedding and he seems to trust her.'

Arjun looked at her in disbelief. 'What if she's on some secret mission to splash our private lives in the newspaper?'

Nitisha's eyes widened. 'Secret mission? Yes, maybe Al-Qaeda has recruited her to do a profile on our caterer. It's a wedding, Bhai, not an episode of *Homeland*.'

'Why aren't you taking this seriously? She's a journalist with a sleazy publication,' Arjun argued.

'Yes, the sleazy publication that gave my spring–summer collection a rave review,' Nitisha reminded him.

'It's not the same thing. That's your professional life, *this* is your wedding—the single most important day of your life. Do you want to become the subject of tabloid gossip?' Arjun demanded, throwing his hands up in frustration.

Surprised by her brother's impassioned response, Nitisha turned to her fiancé for help. Rohan was watching Arjun intently through his rimless glasses. After a long pause, he said, 'If I didn't know any better, I would think you have a personal vendetta against *this* particular journalist.'

'That's impossible, he's never met her,' Nitisha said.

With the most impassive expression he could manage, Arjun said, 'I'm just concerned.'

Rohan raised an eyebrow.

Arjun returned his look.

Confused by the silent exchange between the two men, Nitisha said, 'Bhai, if she didn't sell Vikram's wedding photos to the tabloids, why would she sell mine? Do you seriously believe I'm a bigger celebrity than the vice captain of the Indian cricket team?'

'Not you, but . . . Rohan is,' Arjun finished in a lame attempt to save himself.

Rohan laughed. 'Dude, I'm flattered, but that's not true.'

Nitisha tipped her head and studied her brother carefully. 'Why the sudden paranoia?'

Arjun knew if he pursued this further, his sister would see through him. Actually, he was more worried that *Rohan* would see through him. The man hadn't built an empire from scratch without acquiring the ability to read people along the way. And at that moment, Rohan was watching him with a curious expression that was making Arjun very uncomfortable.

'Never mind,' Arjun muttered, walking towards the bar. 'What can I get you?' he asked Rohan.

'Vodka.'

Arjun turned to his sister. 'Chinky?'

She popped a walnut in her mouth and shook her head. 'I'm on a cleanse till tomorrow.'

Arjun poured Rohan a large vodka and grabbed a beer for himself from the fridge.

'By the way,' Rohan said, taking the glass from Arjun, 'Did you bring the vodka I wanted from duty-free?'

Arjun gave his brother-in-law a disgusted nod. 'You're worth millions, but you still don't want to pay duty on your alcohol? *This* is what the *Economic Times* should be writing about—the thrifty mentality of start-up CEOs.'

'Unlike the others in this room, I wasn't *born* a millionaire. I actually had to work for it,' Rohan countered.

Both Nitisha and Arjun worked really hard at their respective careers, and they knew Rohan respected them for it. But this was just harmless trash talk, so Arjun played along. 'Yes, working with IIT-IIM graduates is *so* tough. Try negotiating the cost of bricks and *sariya* in Pitampura!'

Rohan nodded in agreement. 'With your Hindi skills, I can only imagine how difficult it must be.'

'I'll show you my Hindi skills, *bhen*—' Arjun cut off the expletive, glancing at his sister.

'Not like I haven't heard it all before.' Nitisha sighed, ignoring Arjun's apologetic smile. 'What a family you're marrying into, Rohan. A potty-mouthed brother-in-law, a father-in-law whose only interest in life is golf, and a mother-in-law who will soon drape an orange robe and move out of the house into the SoL ashram on Lodhi Road.'

Both Rohan and Arjun spoke together. 'She's moving out?'

Nitisha chuckled. 'Try not to look so pleased by the thought. And no, she's not.'

Arjun took a sip of his beer. 'A man can hope.'

Rohan sank into the sofa next to his fiancée and draped an arm around her. '*Men.*'

Nitisha punched his arm affectionately.

Arjun groaned. 'Get a room.'

'Very grown-up, Bhai. What in the world are you so cranky about, anyway?' his sister inquired.

'I'm not cranky. I'm just . . . under-slept.'

Rohan pushed his glasses up the bridge of his nose and gave Arjun a sceptical look. 'Dude, I've been hearing that excuse since the day we met. How can you *always* be under-slept? Why don't you just *sleep*?'

Because he couldn't.

'I will, eventually,' Arjun assured Rohan. 'Now tell me,' he said, reaching for the stack of menus in his kitchen drawer, 'what do you guys want for dinner?'

Four days to the wedding

From: Editor, SoL to Soul Magazine <editor@sol.com>
To: all@sol.com
Subject: Newsletter [February 24, 2016]

Jai Priye Ma!

Dear Sisters and Brothers,

This early edition of our newsletter is to celebrate the forthcoming wedding of Nitisha Khanna, daughter of our beloved treasurer, Amy Khanna, and her husband, real estate tycoon Arvind Khanna.

Yesterday marked the beginning of Nitisha's wedding festivities with the Holy Satsang, presided over by Sri Sri Priye Guru Ma herself. Amy initiated the pre-Satsang ceremony by placing twenty-one roses, seven kilos of laddoos, a Tanishq diamond set with matching earrings, and a three-carat diamond ring at the lotus feet of Sri Sri Priye Guru Ma. Priye Ma has generously passed on the gifts to the Science of Living Foundation. However, at Amy's insistence, she has kindly agreed to wear the ring until the culmination of the wedding festivities.

The lovely Divya Sinha, niece of Sri Sri Priye Guru Ma, sang the SoL Prayer, and the Satsang was concluded in one hour. After the Satsang, Priye Ma gave the 'first blessing' (halwa prepared with her very own hands) to Nitisha and her fiancé, Rohan. This brought tears to the eyes of Amy, who is understandably quite emotional about seeing her little bud blossom into a beautiful flower.

The only member of the Khanna family not present at the Satsang was Amy's son, Arjun. The weight of the Khanna empire rests on his able shoulders, and work commitments kept him from attending the Satsang. He conveys his regret at missing the most important event in his sister's wedding festivities. On a lighter note, Arjun is one of the most eligible bachelors in the NCR region, and a little birdie tells us he is single and ready to mingle!

Please find attached some photographs from the event along with links to the press coverage (click on the headline to access the link):

1. Nitisha Khanna and mother wear Khudai [fashiondiva.in]
2. Celebrity spotting at Science of Living satsang [indiajournal.com]
3. Science of Living spends 40 lakhs on single event [indiacults.com]
4. The Khanna–Singhal wedding week begins [newstoday.in]
5. Family rift: Arjun Khanna missing from sister's wedding festivities [page3gossip.com/delhi]
6. Amy Khanna gives SoL's Priye Ma three diamond sets [page3gossip.com/delhi]

Till next time, do remember to touch three lives through the Rhombus of Reliance.

Blessings to you all!

Suchishmito Bandhopadhyay
Editor, SoL to Soul Magazine

'I can't do it,' Arjun told his mother on the phone.

'What do you mean you can't do it?' Amrita gasped.

'Mom, the site is almost a 100 kilometres beyond Gurgaon,' he reasoned. 'How do you expect me to reach New Delhi railway station in an hour?'

'Dahling, you know how much Nani loves you. She'll be devastated if you don't pick her up,' his mother said sweetly.

'She loves Chinky more, send her instead.'

'*Nitisha*,' Amrita said, emphasizing her daughter's name, 'is not allowed to step out of the house until after the wedding. It's a bad omen.'

'That's too bad, because the wedding is at a *hotel*,' he reminded her.

'You know what I mean.'

'Mom, even if I leave immediately, I won't be able to make it to the station in time. Can't you send one of our twenty-three first cousins?' he asked, exasperated.

'They are our guests. It would be rude to send them out for errands,' his mother chided.

'They're just scared of Nani,' he said. 'Why can't Dad go to the station?'

'Because he's supervising the decorations,' Amrita explained.

'That's what the wedding planners are for. In fact, they're charging us a small fortune, tell them to go pick up Nani.'

'You're the only one who can do this,' she insisted.

'What about *you*?' he pointed out.

'Arjun Khanna, your grandmother is seventy-nine years old and she might die any day. Do you really want to send her to her grave wishing you had picked her up from the railway station one last time?' Amrita demanded.

Arjun knew he was fighting a lost battle. Firstly, his mother wouldn't give in till she had convinced him. Secondly, his grandmother was more likely to be annoyed by his tardiness than his absence. And thirdly, Nani was not dying any time soon. Which was the primary reason he didn't want to risk her wrath.

Despite the dramatic picture Amrita had just painted, Nani was hale and hearty. She could drink Arjun under the table any day and knew more bad words in Punjabi than he knew in all the four languages he spoke, combined. She hated air travel because it was 'unsafe', but Arjun suspected the real reason was that airport security didn't allow passengers to carry hip flasks on their person.

'Fine.' Arjun sighed. 'But I'm going to tell her I'm late because of you.'

'No!' Amrita said hastily. 'Just say you had to take Nitisha for a fitting.'

Arjun hung up the phone with a resigned sigh. For a few moments, he studied the ten acres of land in front of him. After three years, the Supreme Court had overturned the high court's order scrapping the land acquisition by Khanna Developers. The petitions of the Haryana farmers had been dismissed and the Khannas had breathed easy. The cost of the land itself was 100 crores, and by the time Arjun was done with it, the units would sell for close to 400 crores.

The February breeze was cool against his face and the sun was shining pleasantly, balancing the chill in the air. Arjun closed his eyes and took a deep breath. It was barely noon and he was already exhausted.

In Mexico the previous week, Arjun and Ali had finished an entire bottle of scotch between the two of them. They had drunk till the sun came up and in a moment of candidness, Ali had told Arjun to 'live a little'. At that time Arjun had simply looked away from his best friend, but he knew exactly what Ali meant.

Arjun had always been a hard worker, but ever since taking over the family business he had become a downright workaholic. On an average, he worked eighteen hours a day, and often woke up in the middle of the night, worried about an email he hadn't sent, a calculation error he thought he'd made, or an approval he'd forgotten to give. Arjun couldn't remember the last time he had slept for more than three hours at a stretch. He loved his job, but he knew he needed to have a life outside of work. He should have helped Chinky plan the wedding, he thought remorsefully.

Maybe, Arjun thought as he slid behind the wheel, his father was right about driving being the most tiring part of the day. But Arjun refused to hire a chauffeur because not only did he hate the idea of being driven around by someone but also because, for some reason, driving seemed to calm him. He rolled down his sleeves and raked a hand through his hair. Nani hated shabbiness and he didn't want to give her another reason to reprimand him.

He started the car and dialled a number on his cell phone. His assistant picked up on the first ring, her voice clear through the car speakers. 'Yes, Arjun?'

'Annie Aunty,' he said, addressing her by the same name he had used since he was five years old. 'I won't be coming in today.'

His dad's former secretary and one of Khanna Developers' first employees, Annabelle Dias came straight to the point. 'Do you want me to hold your calls?'

'Yes. I have to pick up Nani from the station and I doubt she'll take kindly to interruptions.'

He could almost hear Annie Aunty smile through the phone. 'Good luck.'

Arjun hung up and sent his sister a text:

I can bet Nani intentionally planned her travel the day after the satsang.

Chinky replied instantly:

I wouldn't take that bet since I'm the one who changed her tickets. #DontTellAmy

Arjun chuckled to himself. Nani was on their team and he really was looking forward to seeing her.

Three days to the wedding

Risha let the camera drop into her hand strap and relaxed her fingers. One of the guys in her photography group had recommended a hand strap, and at a thousand bucks, it was a great investment. Though Risha's reporting time was 2 p.m., she had arrived at the venue around noon—the extra couple of hours gave her time to wander the grounds, take light readings and test shots.

The venue for the mehndi was the Mezzanine Garden at Khanna Heights, and it was roughly the size of a football field. White canopy drapes arched overhead, and large round tables with lilac spreads and white painted wooden chairs were scattered sporadically in the garden. The bride's seat, a vintage swing, was placed a few feet into the garden, with a white settee and purple brocade bolsters on either side. Lotus flowers floated leisurely in the white fountain at the centre of the garden, and brass lanterns hung from peripheral trees. At the far end of the garden, the adjoining stone amphitheatre steps were accented with strings of purple orchids and large silk cushions in ivory and mauve, and the bar was set up on its cobblestone stage.

Risha took a seat on a step of the amphitheatre right behind the bar, pleased that she could see the entire garden from her vantage point. The sky was slightly overcast and the sun peeked through every few minutes.

Luckily Risha's call with Nitisha had been very encouraging. They had chatted amiably for fifteen minutes, and by the end of the conversation, Risha was convinced that Nitisha was the ideal client. Her response to most things had been 'Totally your call' or 'If you think that will work' or 'I trust your judgment'. In the past, Risha had dealt with a few bridezilla types who insisted on micromanaging everything, so Nitisha giving her complete creative freedom had come as a relief.

Nitisha had mentioned her brother a couple of times in the passing, and both times Risha had found herself holding her breath.

'My brother is hosting the Game Night at his penthouse,' Nitisha said. 'The swimming pool is not very big, but it'll make an interesting backdrop. Bhai picked the theme of the party—he loves old video games.'

One more thing she knew about Arjun Khanna.

Risha heard the white entry gate creak and looked up. The wedding planner, Tanvi, walked in with her clipboard, rattling off instructions into her Bluetooth earpiece. After a couple of minutes, she pressed a small button at her ear and waved at Risha. Risha waved back and jumped off the steps. 'What's up, Shorty?'

At 5'2", Tanvi was several inches shorter than Risha. She had beautiful almond-shaped eyes, a gorgeous dusky complexion and a spunky confidence that often turned the most self-assured men into simpering idiots. And then there was her famous Punjabi temper.

Currently, Tanvi was dressed in a light-green lehenga with a tiny peach blouse and a crinkled silk dupatta draped across her body and knotted at her slim waist. Even though Risha hadn't seen the bride yet, she was sure Tanvi could give Nitisha a run for her money.

Risha glanced down at her own sleeveless yellow top and black jeans. She had tied her long hair in a loose fishtail braid—she couldn't afford random flyaways obstructing her lens—and the only make-up she had worn was some kajal. For a wedding photographer, she looked just fine, but for some reason she suddenly felt grossly underdressed. She felt, in fact, like a Mumbai taxi.

'The usual,' Tanvi said, rolling her eyes. 'Crazy mother, cranky grandmother, pervy cousin.'

Risha gave her a sympathetic look. 'Luckily I only take instructions from the couple.'

'That's what you think. Wait till you meet the rest of them,' Tanvi muttered.

'Damn. And here I was thinking they're a normal bunch,' Risha said.

Tanvi laughed like that was the most ridiculous thing she'd ever heard. 'Earlier today, one of the chachas threw a major temper tantrum because the bar wasn't open.'

'That's not unusual at a Punjabi wedding,' Risha said.

'At 10 a.m., Rish,' Tanvi said, shaking her head in frustration. 'He wanted a drink at ten in the bloody morning!'

'Wow.'

'Yup. And then he threatened to fire me and call the "real professionals" from Shaadi Mubarak.'

'What's Shaadi Mubarak?'

'The fictional wedding-planning company from the movie *Band Baaja Baraat*.'

Risha bit back a smile. 'You should've told him to go ahead.'

'I should've told him to fuck off! Instead, I had to bribe him not to throw the contents of his fruit basket out the window and into the swimming pool, one fruit at a time,' Tanvi said, looking ready to yank her hair out of her scalp.

'What did you bribe him with?'

'One Black Label miniature per fruit,' Tanvi snorted with disgust.

Risha chuckled. 'Look at the bright side, only four more days to go!'

'I'm so tired of this crap. I'm going on a long vacation as soon as this wedding is over.' Tanvi sighed. 'Anyway, Nitisha is nearly ready, so you can go up and take some photos of the family before they all come down here.'

'What floor?'

'Thirty-ninth, the one below the penthouse. Your key card gives you complete access to all floors in the building, including the penthouse lobby,' Tanvi said.

Over the next couple of hours, Risha tirelessly took shots of the family in Amrita and Arvind Khanna's luxurious five-bedroom apartment. Nitisha had introduced her to most of the guests, and thankfully Risha was good with names, because both the bride and groom came from very large families. Risha glanced at the last image of Nitisha twirling in her green ankle-length lehenga as her cousins watched the circumference of the fabric in wonder. She also found an image of Nitisha and Rohan looking out the balcony, engrossed in conversation. Risha had taken that shot, literally, behind their backs.

There were many other images of Nitisha, Rohan, their respective parents and grandparents. Nitisha's Nani was seemingly the chief guest at the wedding—the women of the family tiptoed around her and the men of the family treated her with distant reverence. Nani loved being photographed but never smiled for the photos because she considered it undignified. Instead, she sat erect in her chair and stared blankly into the camera. In every single picture.

The real challenge for Risha at this wedding would be capturing Nani's smile. Or rather, getting Nani to smile in the first place. Risha had slyly managed to take a shot of Nani scowling at her daughter Amrita 'Amy' Khanna. It was evident that the two women couldn't stand each other. As Joshiji, the photo editor at *NT* always said, 'The camera never lies.'

Risha had taken pictures of a few dozen cousins, a score of chachis and masis, a group of close friends and even of the beautiful, but ostentatious, living room of Amrita and Arvind Khanna. Everything and everyone had been clicked several times over *except* the bride's brother. Risha wondered if he really wasn't present or if he just excelled at avoiding her lens. Her question was answered a few minutes later when Rohan's phone rang.

'Yes,' he responded. 'Okay,' he added, glancing at Amrita. 'Got it,' he said, hanging up the phone. He sure was a man of few words, Risha thought.

Rohan turned to his fiancée and whispered, 'Please ask your mother to stop calling your brother. He just got back from the site, he'll get ready and come down to the venue in a while.'

Risha snapped a picture of the exchange and Rohan looked up at her. He smiled sheepishly and Risha captured that too.

'There's no escape, Rohan,' she teased.

Rohan raised his hands up in surrender and shot Risha a smile before following his fiancée.

'Hey you!' a heavy voice called out to Risha.

Nani.

'Yes, Auntyji?'

'Take my photo.'

'Nani,' said one of Nitisha's cousins, 'she is a *candid* photographer. You can't tell her to take photos.'

'What is candy photograafer, Pinku? She has thee camera, she will take thee photo,' Nani said with finality.

'It's okay,' Risha said. 'I can take a few shots, Pinku.'

'*Pankaj*,' he said, clearing his throat. 'Myself Pankaj Sabharwal.'

'Chalo, Candy. Photo *kheecho*,' Nani commanded.

'Sure, Auntyji,' Risha said.

'You can call me Nani like thee others call. And take good photo, this will be my dying photo with thee *haar* on it,' Nani explained.

Risha suppressed a smile and adjusted her lens.

'Okay, Candy, I'm ready. Take it properly.' Nani nodded, sitting up straighter than before and staring blankly into the camera.

'I'll try my best, Nani,' Risha said, swiftly taking a couple of shots.

'Weer you are from?' Nani asked, adjusting the crepe dupatta of her salwar kameez.

'Amritsar,' Risha replied, taking a close-up of Nani's wrinkled fingers on the border of her light-green dupatta.

Nani shot her an interested look. 'Punjabi ho?'

'Hanji.' Risha nodded.

'Surname *batao*?'

'Kohli.'

'Oh, Khatri Punjabi?' Nani beamed, referring to her caste.

'Hanji,' Risha said.

'We are also same-to-same,' Nani said. 'But Khanna is superior to Kohli.'

'Nani!' Nitisha sputtered, appearing behind her grandmother with an appalled expression. 'I think that's enough talk about the Punjabi caste hierarchy.' She mouthed 'sorry' to Risha, and Risha mouthed back 'it's okay'.

'But I am only telling thee truth,' Nani said innocently.

'As always,' Nitisha muttered. 'Nani, we need to go down to the garden now, Pinku will take you. Risha, I'll see you downstairs?' she hinted, heading towards the door.

'Sure, I'll be right down,' Risha assured Nitisha before turning to her grandmother. 'I'll see you later, Nani.'

'You diddunt show me thee photo, Candy.'

Risha bent down and showed Nani her camera screen. Nani looked pleased. 'Pinku, tell Mummy to use this photo when I die.'

Pinku gave Nani an earnest Indian-style nod, then turned to Risha with a shy smile. 'Actually, Pinku is my pet name. My good name is Pankaj Sabharwal,' he explained, handing her a visiting card from a chrome cardholder.

'Nice to meet you, Pankaj,' Risha smiled, absently shoving the card into her pocket. 'I better head downstairs, see you around!'

'Okay, yes. Thank you. Same here, I mean. Okay, see you.' Pinku blushed, watching Risha disappear.

Ladkiyon ki tarah kyun sharma raha hai?' Nani asked Pinku in a clipped tone. Chastened, he took her hand and escorted her to the elevator, his face a bright shade of pink.

Downstairs in the garden, Nani found a table near the bar and ordered herself a large scotch on the rocks. She looked at her Cartier watch, a gift from the late maharaja of Patiala, and grimaced at the time. Her favourite grandson was late again.

An hour later, Arjun and his father stepped out of the elevator, into the Mezzanine Garden.

'Dad, this is exactly why I've been telling you we should outsource construction,' Arjun said grimly. 'DLF has done it, we should too.'

This morning, Khanna Developers' in-house contractor, Mukesh Yadav, had dropped a bomb on Arjun: the workers were going on a three-week strike.

The news had shocked Arjun, who, after the last board meeting, had promised Yadav a revision in contract rates post the completion of this project. As a show of good faith, Arjun had even built the cost into the P&L for the next project. At that time, Yadav had agreed to it, so what had changed now?

'My hands are tied, Bhaiyaji,' Yadav had said sincerely. 'I tried to convince the men, but they are just not agreeing. What can I do?'

As the liaison between the workers and Khanna Developers, Yadav was the only one who *could* do something. Slab-laying work was already on hold due to a delay in sand supplies, and the strike would only push things back further. Arjun had visited Yadav's house and spent an hour trying to reason with him, but the man hadn't budged.

'If it were up to me, this strike would never happen,' Yadav assured him. Arjun had declined Yadav's invitation to stay for lunch, and left only when Yadav promised to attend Chinky's wedding.

Each day that construction was on hold resulted in a huge monetary loss, not to mention an extension in the deadline. Arjun had worked very hard on Khanna Developers' reputation as the 'on time' builder, and he wasn't about to let an unscheduled strike damage it.

Not wanting to cause his father additional stress, Arjun said, 'Never mind, I'll talk to Yadav and figure it out.'

Arvind slapped him on the back. 'It's Chinky's wedding that we should prioritize. Let's deal with this on Monday, beta.'

For his father's benefit, Arjun gave a small smile which widened into a genuine grin as soon as he walked into the garden and spotted his sister. 'Hey,' he said, engulfing her in a hug.

'Careful!' Nitisha said, showing him her hennaed hands.

'Sorry,' he said, stepping back. 'You look nice.'

'Thanks, so do you. Where did you get that fabulous kurta?' She winked.

'A highly overpriced store called Khudai. But I didn't pay for it, so who cares?' Arjun shrugged.

'Very funny,' Nitisha said. 'All okay at the site?'

'More or less, don't worry about it. Do you want a drink?' Arjun asked.

'Orange juice.'

'With?'

'Nothing. I'm not drinking until tomorrow night, remember?'

Arjun shook his head in resignation. 'Okay, I'll send you an orange juice.'

He had merely walked a few feet towards the bar when he heard his mother's excited squeal. 'Arjun dahling, you're finally here! There's someone I want you to meet.'

Arjun gave her a brief hug. 'Hi, Mom.'

'This,' Amrita said, gesturing to the girl next to her, 'is Divya.'

Mom was hoping to introduce you to someone.

Arjun groaned internally and turned towards the skinny girl beside his mother. 'Hi, Divya, nice to meet you.'

'Same here,' Divya said, sounding bored.

Arjun studied her fauxhawk, gothic make-up, khadi tank top and black dhoti, right down to the black toenails peeking out from her Kolhapuri chappals. Divya was the exact opposite of the kind of girl he would expect his mother to set him up with, Arjun thought in surprise.

'Divya *Sinha*,' his mother emphasized.

'Any relation to Priya Sinha?' Arjun drawled distastefully.

'I'm her niece,' Divya said.

That explained it.

'Divya is a very talented singer,' Amrita gushed. 'She sings in all the satsangs *and* she's in a band.'

'What kind of band?' Arjun asked politely.

'Carnatic fusion,' Divya said.

'Such a talented girl. And so pretty, no?' Amrita beamed at her son. Arjun shot her a warning look, but she ignored it. 'Divya just moved here from Bangalore and she doesn't know anyone. Why don't you show her around, Arjun?' she suggested, with a sly smile.

Subtlety was not his mother's strong point.

'Divya,' Arjun began, more out of good manners than genuine interest, 'I was just heading to the bar. Would you like to join me?'

'Sure,' Diyva said.

'After you.'

A few minutes later, Arjun realized that hanging out with Divya wasn't so bad. She only spoke when spoken to, and even then her responses were limited to monosyllables or short sentences. And the best part was that she seemed as uninterested in him as he was in her. Arjun caught sight of his masi's sons and waved them over.

'Arjun Bhaiya, *kaise ho*?' Pinku said with a wide grin.

'Good, yaar. How are you guys? Meet Divya. Divya, these are my cousins, Pinku and Minku.'

'Myself Pankaj Sabharwal,' Pinku said, adjusting his tie and reaching into his pocket for a visiting card. 'And this is my younger brother, Manoj. Nice to meet you.'

'Same here,' Divya said, with the same lack of zest with which she had greeted Arjun.

'I have to go say hello to Nani,' Arjun said. 'Will you excuse me?'

Divya gave him an indifferent shrug and Arjun turned towards the bartender. Given how late he was, he would feel better equipped with Nani's favourite drink. He spotted Rohan at Nani's table and gave him a nod. Rohan threw him a you're-so-dead look and said, *'Nani, aa gaya aapka laadla.'*

Arjun bent down to touch her feet. 'Sorry, I'm late.'

'No, no. *Behen ki shaadi* only, nothing important,' Nani said, crossing her arms over her chest.

'I was at the site, Nani. There was a lot of traffic on—'

'Arrey, bhai, you are *ladki wala.* You can come and go whenever you want,' Nani said, deadpan.

Rohan grinned at Arjun from behind Nani, clearly enjoying the admonishing his future brother-in-law was receiving. He was forced to check his grin abruptly when Nani turned to him. 'Haina, Rohan?'

'Uh, yes, Nani. I mean, no. Of course, he shouldn't be late. It's disrespectful to his guests,' Rohan said solemnly.

'Nani ka chamcha,' Arjun muttered under his breath. Out of ammunition, he placed the glass in front of Nani and attempted to change the subject. 'I brought you a drink. Speaking of which, have you told Rohan about the origins of the Patiala peg?'

Nani took a large swig from the glass. 'Thee maharaja of Patiala hosted a dinner for thee Irish tent-pegging team on thee night before their big match against Patiala. Thee bartenders were instructed to offer extra-large pegs of 120 ml to thee Irishmen. They all woke up with bad *hen*govers and thee Patiala team won thee match.'

Though he had heard the story before, Rohan feigned protest. 'But that's cheating, Nani!'

'Patiala maharajas always got their way,' Nani said matter-of-factly.

Arjun and Rohan exchanged a look. They had both heard the rumour about Nani being the mistress of one of the Patiala kings.

'Rohan,' Nani began, 'Vikram Walia *kab aayega*? I want to talk to him about cricket. Back in thee day I attended many cricket matches in thee royal pavilion of thee Patiala cricket ground.'

Arjun had a sudden vision of a black-and-white photograph of an unsmiling lady in a silk sari. Nani had shown it to him in a coffee-table book about Patiala royalty the summer before he moved to New York. The photograph was captioned 'The Maharaja's Guest', and the lady was wearing a watch that looked all too similar to the one Nani was wearing right now.

'He's in Mumbai for the day, but he'll be here tomorrow,' Rohan answered, shifting in his chair.

'He is so *hend*some and dashing!' Nani gushed.

Vikram Walia *was* a good-looking dude, Arjun thought objectively. But Arjun wasn't keen on pursuing a discussion on cricketers—let alone Patiala royalty—so he grabbed his phone to distract his grandmother. 'Let's take a picture, Nani.'

'What is this phone-shone photo? Click properly for thee *el*bum. *Candy ko bulao*!'

Arjun turned to her with a puzzled look. 'Who is Candy?'

Risha turned around at the sound of her new alias. Ever since Nani had christened her 'Candy', the entire wedding party had been addressing her by that name.

'What happened, Shruti?' Risha asked Rohan's thirteen-year-old niece.

'Candy Didi, Nani is calling you,' Shruti said, pointing in the direction of Nani's table.

'Okay, I'll be there in a second,' Risha responded, guzzling a small bottle of Bisleri water. She pointed her camera at Nani's table, hoping to catch the old lady in a candid moment, when she spotted Arjun. Her breath caught in her throat as she saw him laugh at something his grandmother said. Risha zoomed in on his face and took a burst shot. His eyes crinkled at the corners and his perfect white teeth gleamed in the sun. She wondered if he had braces as a kid or if he was born with that flawless smile.

She shook her head, trying to clear her thoughts as she walked towards their table. She hid her face behind her camera and took a couple of shots, preparing herself for the moment they finally met again.

'Hi,' she said softly.

The smile vanished from Arjun's face. 'Ms Kohli, I presume,' he said formally.

Baffled by his lack of warmth and recognition, Risha narrowed her eyes. When Arjun continued to look at her blankly, she returned his greeting with cool reserve. 'Mr Khanna.'

'You both are a match,' Nani said.

'What?' Arjun turned to his grandmother in complete shock.

'You are weering chikan, she is also weering chikan,' Nani said, pointing to the chikankari embroidery on his kurta.

Arjun looked at Risha's yellow top and then down at his own smoky-white kurta. Comprehension dawned upon him. 'Oh.'

'Maybe they planned it in advance, Nani,' Rohan suggested casually.

Arjun shot Rohan a dirty look before turning to Risha. 'Can you take a few pictures?'

'Sure,' Risha said nonchalantly. Over the next few minutes, she took their photos, instructing them to look this way and pose that way. The more uncomfortable Arjun appeared with all the posing, the more Risha found herself enjoying the photography session.

'Chalo, enough for now,' Nani said. 'Arjun, get a drink for Candy.'

'I can't, Nani. I'm on duty,' Risha said, pointing to her camera.

Nani waved off her concern. *Duty-shuty toh chalti rahegi.*'

'I really can't,' Risha said firmly.

'You can and you must,' Nani insisted.

Realizing Nani wouldn't relent, Risha acquiesced. 'Maybe towards the end of the evening.'

'Okay, but don't leave without having a drink with me,' Nani warned.

'I won't,' Risha promised.

'Arjun, go get Candy some coffee instead,' Nani said. Arjun gritted his teeth but stood up.

Risha shook her head. 'I just had coffee,' she lied. 'I have to take a few solo shots of Nitisha, I'll see you all in a bit.' Before Nani could voice any further objections, Risha disappeared.

She walked all the way across the crowded garden and stepped into the elevator. As the doors closed, she pushed the button for the sixth floor and exhaled deeply.

What had just happened? Was this cold, aloof man the same Arjun who had exchanged his dessert with her and teased her with silly nicknames a mere three days ago? She couldn't believe this was the same person she had spent the last forty-eight hours stalking online. And she certainly couldn't guess the reason for the sudden shift in his attitude. Maybe it was because they were no longer equals. He owned the building in which she stood, along with half the city. And she was just a wedding photographer. But he had known that on the flight and he didn't act like such a rich snob then. Had she really misjudged him so much?

Get your act together, Risha. You're a goddamn professional.

Risha stepped on to the balcony and changed the lens of her camera, wanting to take a few aerial shots of the gathering before it got too dark. Little splashes of colour peeked through the white drapes in the garden. Nitisha sat with her green lehenga spread around her and the henna artists pored over her legs, mehndi flowing from the tips of their little henna cones. Risha zoomed in on the setting, using the drapes to frame her shot. She nodded at the output, pleased with the picturesque scene she had just captured. A few minutes later, her silent session was interrupted by her phone. She answered it, sighing pre-emptively. 'Yes, Rishabh?'

'How's it going, Kohli?' her friend said cheerily.

'I'm working. What do you want?' Risha asked impatiently, balancing the phone between her ear and shoulder, as she carefully positioned her camera on the stone baluster.

'Do you want to meet for dinner tonight? I'm at a shoot in Gurgaon till eight o'clock, but we can stop at the new sushi place in Cyber Hub on our way home,' Rishabh said.

'I don't know what time I'll get off.'

'Come on, Kohli. I haven't seen your face in months!' he whined.

'We had dinner together *last night*,' she pointed out.

'Having kathi rolls outside your building while Tyagiji gives me death stares doesn't count as "having dinner together",' he groaned. 'Besides, the bartender at the sushi place has an ass that won't quit.'

'So you need a wingwoman?' she said dryly.

'Who better to back up a gay guy than a straight best friend?' he chortled.

'I honestly don't know when I'll be free. Let me text you in a bit,' she said, hanging up and sliding her phone into her pocket. Her fingers brushed against a small rectangular piece of paper: Pinku's visiting card. On the left corner of the card was a woman dressed in a bright red Patiala salwar and in the centre were the words 'Salwar Hi Salwar' in purple Comic Sans. Under that it said 'Pankaj Sabharwal, Proprietor' in bright magenta.

Risha laughed out loud, then took a quick picture of the card with her cell phone and texted it to Nidhi with the caption 'Design for dummies'.

Risha wrapped up her last shot and grabbed her things, heading back to the venue. As the elevator opened to the mezzanine floor, Risha was greeted by a loud cheer.

'There you are!' a lady with blonde highlights said, clapping her hands together. 'Amy, she's here!'

Amrita turned to her in delight. 'Candy, dahling! Just the person I was looking for. Can you take a few pictures of our satsang group for the SoL Facebook profile page?'

So much for candid photography.

'Sure,' Risha said.

Another lady with perfect curls and a mole above her lip turned to Risha. 'Yes, take some nice selfies.'

'You want me to be in the photo?' Risha asked, puzzled.

The fake blonde looked at Risha like the idea was preposterous. 'Of course not, silly! Take selfies of *us*.'

Resisting the temptation to roll her eyes, Risha suggested, 'Why don't we go to the amphitheatre, we can get some great shots there.'

Amrita gathered her troop of kitty-party aunties and marched them to the amphitheatre. After twenty minutes of 'I look fat in that photo, delete it', 'My hair looks frizzy, delete it' and 'I have lipstick on my teeth, delete it', Risha was left with three 'approved' photos in her camera.

'Great job, ladies!' Risha said with fake enthusiasm, helping one of them step down on to the stage.

Amrita took Risha aside by the arm and said in a covert whisper, 'Listen, Candy, I need you to take some couple photos.'

'Of Nitisha and Rohan?' Risha asked.

'No, no. Of Arjun and Divya,' Amrita clarified.

Risha's face fell. 'Oh.' She regained her composure and nodded. 'Of course.'

So he was dating a girl called Divya. Suddenly it all made sense. On the flight he'd been chattering away with Risha, but now that his girlfriend was here, he didn't even want to acknowledge her existence. Typical male, Risha thought, irrationally blaming the entire gender for his actions.

Screw him. She was a professional and there's no way she would let his icy arrogance affect her.

Because it didn't.

'In fact, Amy,' Risha said with a resolute smile, 'there's a beautiful peepul tree on the east corner of the garden. Tanvi's team has hung a few lanterns from its branches, and I think it would make a lovely romantic backdrop around sunset. Can you bring them both there in an hour?'

Amrita's eyes lit up. 'Of course! Thanks, Candy, you're a doll.' She then walked off to air-kiss a group of women her age.

Risha took out her phone and typed a quick message to Nidhi:

When are you getting here?

Nidhi replied:

Don't kill me but I'm not coming today. I'm working half day tomorrow though, wanna come over for lunch?

Risha groaned and typed back:

> Okay, but please remember to remove the dagger
> from my back before we eat.

Then she sent a text to Rishabh:

> Pick me up from Khanna Heights around 9.

Risha headed back up the steps of the amphitheatre. As Arjun had pointed out on the flight, she *needed* to take his photos to get paid. She purposefully took a seat on the step behind the bar. The height gave her a good view and flexibility, and she was out of the line of sight of the guests. Risha pointed her camera determinedly in the direction of the bar and started shooting.

'Where are you taking me?' Arjun asked his mother impatiently.

'Just come with me, dahling,' Amrita said, a mysterious smile on her face. 'Stand under this tree.'

Arjun looked up at the tree cluelessly. 'Why?'

'You'll thank me later.' Amrita winked as Divya appeared behind her.

'Hi,' Divya said.

Arjun narrowed his eyes. 'What's going on?'

'I don't know,' Divya said, and he thought she added under her breath, 'and I don't care.'

'Hello, lovebirds!' Risha said brightly. 'If you'll just step a little closer and look at each other—'

'Is this supposed to be funny?' Arjun asked in a bored tone.

Risha looked from Arjun to Amrita and shrugged. 'I'm just doing my job.'

'What the hell does that mean?' Arjun raged.

Risha threw back her shoulders. 'There's no need to raise your voice, Mr Khanna. Your mother asked me to take pictures of you both, and that's what I'm doing.'

'Mom! What the hell is this?' Arjun exploded.

Amrita gave him an over-bright smile. 'Just some photos for the SoL newsletter, dahling.'

'Don't be ridiculous.' Arjun scowled. 'Divya, my mother has clearly taken leave of her senses. I apologize on her behalf.'

With that, he turned around and left.

Risha looked up at the sky and pinched the bridge of her nose. She could really use a break from this lunatic asylum.

An hour later, Risha sat at a table surrounded by Nitisha's and Rohan's cousins. One of them had asked her to share funny experiences from the weddings she had shot, and after a few minutes, a small crowd had gathered at the table, hungry for more amusing anecdotes.

Risha dipped her samosa into her masala chai and took a bite, continuing her story, 'So the bride's chacha decided to use mehndi to dye his hair. Unfortunately, his hair turned completely orange!' Risha chomped on her samosa, waiting for the laughter to subside. 'The worst part is, he had also used the mehndi on his ear hair!' The crowd erupted in laughter.

A few feet away at the bar, Arjun watched Risha laugh. He remembered hearing that story on the flight. Apparently, he wasn't the only one she'd been regaling with funny wedding stories, he thought with some annoyance. He watched the rays of the setting sun stream on her messy braid, making her hair appear like spun gold. He wondered how her hair looked undone, and his grasp on his Hoegaarden bottle tightened unwittingly. Vexed with the direction of his thoughts, he dragged his gaze away from Risha.

Rohan was watching him with an amused smile.

'What?' Arjun snapped.

'Nothing,' Rohan said, taking a sip of his beer. 'When do your college friends get here?'

'Angad will be here tomorrow, the other two won't be able to make it,' Arjun said.

'Why not?'

'Karan is saving his leave for his own wedding.'

'What about Ali?' Rohan asked.

'He needs to attend the swearing-in ceremony of the new PM,' Arjun explained.

'Talk about a shitty excuse,' Rohan joked.

Arjun laughed. 'That's Ali for you.'

They sipped their beers in silence until Rohan said, 'Is there a reason you keep glancing at that table?'

Arjun's hand froze mid-air. 'What?'

Rohan smiled and took another sip of his beer.

Arjun's brows snapped together in irritation. 'Is there something you're trying to ask me?'

Rohan came straight to the point. 'Do you know her from before?'

'Do I know *who* from before?' Arjun stalled.

'Do you know "Ms Kohli" from before?'

Arjun briefly considered lying. Since Rohan had started seeing Chinky a couple of years ago, he and Arjun had become good friends. Their management styles were strikingly similar and they often turned to each other for professional advice. Arjun relied on Rohan's business acumen while making important decisions and also respected him immensely as a person. Rohan had a strong work ethic, but he had an even stronger sense of family values. And above all, he made Chinky happier than Arjun had ever seen her.

So Arjun nodded. 'Vaguely. How did you guess?'

'For one thing, your extreme reaction to her being a journalist,' Rohan said. 'But mainly the fact that you keep staring at her.'

'I met her on the flight back from LA. We spoke for a few hours and I thought we had a connection, but . . .' he trailed off.

Rohan patiently waited for him to continue.

'But she lied about being a journalist,' Arjun said.

'She *lied*?' Rohan asked.

'We spoke for hours and she never mentioned it.'

Rohan frowned. 'Dude, that's not the same thing.'

'Lying by omission is basically as bad as lying,' Arjun argued.

Rohan took off his glasses and blew on the lens, before sliding them back on. 'Did Nitisha ever tell you about the first email we received from Risha?'

'No.'

'It contained a brief profile of hers.'

'And?' Arjun asked, not sure where Rohan was going with this.

'Something on the lines of "I don't have much professional experience, and though this is not my full-time job, I'm very passionate about it. I've only shot four weddings till date, etc., etc." It *did* mention that she works at *News Today* and that it wouldn't interfere with her commitment to our wedding. And the email ended with a line about a "20 per cent friends and family discount" because we know Vikram and Nidhi.'

'So the discount is what won you over, you cheap bastard?'

Rohan chuckled. 'Yes. But mainly the fact that she was so forthcoming about being a novice. She could've concealed her inexperience, instead she volunteered the truth.'

'Maybe she thought you would find out from Vikram anyway,' Arjun pointed out.

'It's possible. But this morning she showed up two hours before she was supposed to. She's going to get paid no matter what, but she came early anyway. To me, that shows integrity. I don't really know much about this girl, but I don't think she's a liar.'

'You're just biased because Vikram referred her,' Arjun said, aware that Rohan was blindly loyal to his childhood friend.

'That's part of it,' Rohan admitted candidly. 'But she seems like a straight shooter to me. And I think your general dislike for journalists is clouding your opinion of her.'

Arjun rubbed his thumb on the rim of his beer bottle. 'What are you suggesting?'

'Talk to Candy.'

Arjun laughed. 'Who came up with that name?'

'Nani, who else?' Rohan said, shaking his head.

'How?' Arjun wondered out loud.

'Ask her yourself,' Rohan said, pointing to the table where Nani now sat next to Risha. The crowd had dissipated, likely due to Nani's appearance, and Risha and Nani were in an animated discussion. Arjun stepped closer to their table and he could hear traces of the conversation.

'Patiala ka *bed*minton champion hai,' Nani boasted, referring to his cousin Gurvinder, '*pat* name Guri'. 'You should see his cock collection—*so* big!'

Risha choked on her samosa and Arjun swallowed his laughter.

'If you marry him, he will keep you *set*isfied,' Nani continued.

Whoa! Was Nani matchmaking? What was wrong with the women in his family?

Arjun took another involuntary step towards their table.

'In Patiala, my dear, thee peg is not thee *only* thing that is large,' Nani said, looking delighted. Arjun's eyes widened as Nani went on, 'Patiala men have thee biggest—'

'Nani!' Arjun sputtered, practically leaping into the chair next to hers.

Nani looked up at him and her face broke into a wide smile. Risha looked at her in shock and slyly reached for the camera, hoping Nani's smile would stay in place long enough for Risha to push the click button.

'Tell Candy why Guri is perfect for her,' Nani said to her grandson.

Arjun rolled up his sleeves. 'He's not.'

'*Kyun?*' Nani scowled.

Risha sighed, putting her camera back down. *So close.*

Arjun looked at Nani in mock astonishment. 'What about Harinder, "*pat* name Harry"? The most eligible bachelor of Bhatinda and winner of the last annual bullock cart race.'

Nani seemed excited. 'Crect! Herry is also an exlent option.'

Arjun gave Risha a playful smile, but she looked away, addressing Nani instead. 'I have to go.'

'What go-go all thee time? You need a break,' Nani said.

'I just took a break,' Risha said politely, standing up. 'I have to take a few night shots of the couple.'

'Take them and come back, we will wait. Then we will talk about Herry,' Nani said firmly.

Risha felt an inexplicable surge of affection for Nani. She was just a lonely old lady who craved company and, raunchy comments notwithstanding, reminded Risha a little of her own grandmother. So Risha nodded. 'Okay, Nani.'

She thought she felt Arjun's gaze on her as she walked away, but when she turned around he was fiddling with the label of his beer bottle, peeling it off absent-mindedly. Risha glanced at her watch; it was already 8 p.m. and Rishabh would be coming for her soon. Time to wrap up this party.

Unfortunately, at a quarter-to-ten, the party had still not 'wrapped up', and Risha received her third, and most irate, phone call from Rishabh. 'What the hell, Kohli? I've been waiting for an hour. I'm starving!' he yelled.

Risha held the phone away from her ear. She had been instructed by Amrita to stay back and take pictures of the legendary Sri Sri Priye Guru Ma. The priestess was supposed to show up at 8.30 p.m. to shower the couple with her blessings, but she was more than an hour late. And the worst part was that she lived on the seventeenth floor of Khanna Heights. Risha had half the mind to knock down her door. After all, she did have an all-access key card.

'I'm sorry, Rishabh, this is taking longer than I expected. I'll call you back in a minute, I promise,' Risha said apologetically. She walked over to the table where Nitisha was seated with her immediate family and leaned down. 'Can I talk to you?'

Nitisha looked concerned. 'All okay?'

'Yes, it will only take a minute,' Risha said.

'Of course.' Nitisha stood up, hands akimbo to avoid smudging her mehndi. Nani cocked her head, trying to eavesdrop.

'Um, the thing is, this is, uh, embarrassing, but I have a small favour to ask,' Risha said clumsily.

'What is it?' Nitisha asked.

'My friend is downstairs and, uh, he's my ride home. We were supposed to have dinner together and he's been waiting in the car for a while. I don't know how long Priye Ma will be, so, um, is it okay if he comes up and waits here for a bit?'

'Oh my god, of course! I'm so sorry to put you in this situation, Risha,' Nitisha said, visibly contrite. 'Please invite him up for dinner. I'm so sorry for ruining your plans!'

'No, it's not your fault. I should've accounted for delays,' Risha said, relieved. 'Thanks, Nitisha, I appreciate it!'

'Absolutely, it would be a pleasure to have him. I could speak to him if you want?'

'That's okay, I'll go down and get him,' Risha said.

'Okay, great!' Nitisha smiled. 'Bring him over to our table.'

Risha nodded gratefully. The moment she reached Rishabh's car, he switched on the headlights and started the ignition, revving loudly for effect. Risha shook her head and tapped on his window.

'What now?' he snapped. 'Let's go before I die!'

'Um, you need to come up,' Risha said helplessly.

His eyes flashed murder. 'Why?'

'I need some more time, so I thought you could come up and hang around for a bit,' Risha suggested. When his glare intensified, she added, 'With Nitisha Khanna.'

He looked slightly mollified. 'Go on.'

'I told Nitisha you were waiting in the car, so she asked me to invite you up for dinner,' she explained.

Rishabh jumped out of the car and enveloped Risha in a hug. 'You're the best, Kohli!'

'I know, but please behave yourself. No flirting with anyone, no inappropriate jokes and no scandalizing old people by mentioning your sexual orientation,' Risha instructed.

'Don't worry, I'll be on my best behaviour,' he promised.

'And do *not* bring up your professional aspirations,' she warned.

In the lobby, Rishabh spent a good five minutes on his appearance, primping his perfectly styled hair one strand at a time. He pouted at his reflection in the large mirror, admiring his jaw from various angles. Risha stood with her hands on her hips, tapping her foot impatiently. Another minute passed and she cleared her throat loudly.

'Okay, okay, let's go,' Rishabh said, brushing an imaginary piece of lint off his tan leather jacket.

'Are you sure? Because we have all day.'

'How is it,' he said, striding into the elevator, 'that you always manage to make time for sarcasm, Kohli?'

As they approached Nitisha's table, Risha saw Arjun frown. She squirmed under his piercing gaze. Why did he have to make her feel so unwelcome?

Nitisha greeted Rishabh warmly, and he air-kissed both her cheeks. 'Enchanted to meet you! You are by far the most gorgeous bride I've ever seen and—'

Risha cut him off with a warning look. 'Apologies for the intrusion, this is my friend—'

'*Good friend*,' Rishabh corrected.

'Good friend,' Risha said through gritted teeth, 'Rishabh.'

Rohan saw the glint of recognition in Arjun's eyes. Both men stood up and shook Rishabh's hand. Arvind Khanna picked up a platter from the table and held it out to Rishabh. 'Help yourself, beta.'

Rishabh shot him a grateful look and gathered three kebabs in a single toothpick.

Risha covered her face with her palm.

Nani gave Rishabh a suspicious once-over. 'How do you know Candy?'

'Who is—'

'She means me,' Risha interjected.

Rishabh gave her a look. *Sounds like a tramp's name.*

Risha shook her head. *Don't ask.*

Arjun watched the exchange between them in brooding silence.

'*Candy* and I went to school together in Amritsar,' Rishabh said.

Nani arched an eyebrow. 'Punjabi ho?'

'Hanji, Auntyji,' Rishabh confirmed.

Nani's next question was cut off by a loud song blaring through the speakers. She covered her ears with her hands, just as Nitisha stood up. 'That's the SoL prayer. I'm guessing Priye Ma has arrived. Come on people, let's get this over with!'

Nitisha walked towards the entrance, accompanied by her father and future in-laws. Risha turned to Rishabh and mouthed 'behave' before following Nitisha.

Rohan stood up reluctantly and looked at Arjun. 'Coming?'

Arjun shook his head. 'No, thanks.'

'Not everyone has the privilege of receiving Priye Ma's blessings in person,' Rohan pointed out.

'Priye Ma ki,' Arjun said under his breath. Rohan sniggered at the truncated curse, but followed the group to the entrance.

With uncharacteristic patience, Nani watched Rishabh wolf down an entire plate of kebabs, a bowl of jalapeño poppers and a martini. Impressed, she continued her interrogation of their new guest. 'Rishabh?'

'Hanji, Auntyji?'

'You can call me Nani.'

'Okay, Nani.'

'Surname batao?'

'Kapoor,' he answered.

Nani grunted.

Arjun looked at her. 'What?'

She leaned in and replied in a sullen whisper, 'Kapoor is superior to Khanna.'

Behind his ivory serviette, Rishabh smiled.

Arjun turned his attention to Rishabh. 'What do you do?'

'I'm a model.'

Of course.

'What do *you* do?' Rishabh asked casually.

'I'm in real estate,' Arjun said dryly, pointing to the skyscraper behind him.

Nani gave Arjun a curious look. Her grandson had many flaws, but immodesty was not one of them. She turned to Rishabh and asked bluntly, 'How close you both are? You and Candy?'

Rishabh heard Arjun's sharp intake of breath and he replied, 'Oh, I would say we're quite close.' Arjun leaned forward ever so slightly and Rishabh added, '*Very* close.'

If he hadn't spent a large part of his life observing male body language, Rishabh might have missed the imperceptible clenching of Arjun's jaw. But he had, and he didn't.

Interesting.

'It's a wrap, ladies!' Risha said, addressing the SoL group.

Amrita Khanna, who had been in a state of hypnotic obeisance since Priye Ma had entered the garden, stared at her retreating form and said softly, 'Great woman. Great woman.'

Risha nodded, even though she couldn't disagree more. With her long hair extensions, blue contact lenses and thick winged eyeliner, Priye Ma looked more like an older version of Celina Jaitley than a spiritual leader. Plus, she had a perpetual creepy smile painted on her face. Risha could bet her camera that Priye Ma's jaw was really hurting by this time.

Risha turned to Amrita. 'I'm gonna go.'

Amrita came out of her catatonic state long enough to give Risha a distracted smile.

Risha walked towards Rishabh's table, thinking that she couldn't get out of this madhouse fast enough. She had a mild headache, partly from hunger, but mostly from Priye Ma's cryptic sermon. For some reason the woman kept using arcane alliterations like 'Pentagon of Perfection' or 'Truce Trapezium' or 'Heptagon of Happiness', and her followers reverently nodded along to Priye Ma's pearls of wisdom.

As far as Risha was concerned, it was random geometrical jargon combined with unsubstantial content and unimpressive delivery. Or, as she had started referring to it in her head, 'Triangle of Total Crap'.

It was evident that the sole reason the Khannas entertained Priye Ma was to humour Amy Khanna. The bride was definitely a non-believer, because at one point Priye Ma had asked the couple to 'be open to a three-way with god', Nitisha's shoulders had shaken with suppressed mirth. Rohan had a small coughing fit to cover for his fiancée.

Risha sank into the chair between Arjun and Rishabh, and reached for the paneer tikka residue on the platter in front of her.

Arjun tipped his head in the direction of the SoL gathering. 'So, are you going to convert?'

Risha picked up a slice of grilled capsicum between her index finger and thumb, before turning to Arjun with sham gravity. 'Of course, I just signed the application form.'

Rishabh caught Arjun's alarmed expression and chuckled. 'She's joking.'

Arjun flashed Risha a lazy smile. 'You had me worried for a moment, Ms Kohli.'

Risha grinned and popped a grilled tomato into her mouth.

'Worried about what?' Nitisha said, plonking herself into the seat across from Risha's.

'Risha is thinking of joining SoL,' Arjun said, beckoning a waiter with a slight nod of his head.

Nani scoffed. 'Most worst organization.'

'Just "worst",' Nitisha corrected.

'Crect.' Nani nodded. 'Just most worst organization.'

Rohan came up behind Nitisha. 'Worst organization with an annual turnover of 200 crores, anyway.'

Risha looked up in shock. 'Really?' she asked, reaching for the wooden skewer, tempted to lick the masala off it.

Arjun turned to the waiter who had magically appeared at his side, and gestured to Risha. 'A plate of paneer tikka for the lady.'

Risha shook her head. 'Thanks, but I think we better leave.'

'Stay for dinner,' Arjun suggested politely.

'It's getting late and we have to drive to Vasant Kunj,' Risha explained, standing up.

'Sit!' Nani ordered. 'You diddunt drink thee drink you promised me.'

Rishabh was off his chair in a flash, pushing Risha back into the chair by her shoulders. 'Yes, sweetie, you should have a drink. You look *exhausted*.'

Risha's mouth hung open. Rishabh hadn't called her by her first name in ten years and now he was calling her 'sweetie'?

'Deepak!' Nani summoned the bartender. '*Patiala lao sab ke liye.*'

Rishabh massaged Risha's shoulders gently and she shrugged his hands off. 'What are you doing?' she hissed, with a smile pasted on her face.

'You just look so tired, babe,' he said, looking straight at Arjun.

'Oh, I didn't realize you guys are—' Nitisha said.

Rishabh pre-empted her question with a nod. 'Risha and Rishabh. Cute, no?'

'No,' Arjun said shortly.

Nitisha glared at him and he shrugged.

'He's just joking,' Nitisha clarified with a forced laugh.

Risha shot Rishabh a murderous look and he reluctantly returned to his seat. A waitress arrived with their drinks, and Rohan—god bless him, Risha thought—asked her to serve dinner as well. Risha rubbed the goosebumps on her arms, it was much colder than she had expected. Rishabh stood up again and she threw him an exasperated look. 'What now?'

He took off his jacket and draped it over Risha's shoulders. 'Just keeping you warm.'

Risha stared at him in blank shock. If they were ever stranded in Antarctica, Risha had no doubt that Rishabh

Kapoor would eat her alive to ensure his own survival. Yet, here he was, offering her his jacket on a chilly winter evening. What the hell had gotten into him today?

'Have you been drinking?' Risha blurted.

'Just a little, sweetie,' Rishabh said with an indulgent smile.

Arjun leaned back in his chair and crossed his arms, his eyes narrowed. Risha took a large sip of her drink and stared at his muscular forearms. Following her gaze, Nani suddenly asked, 'Candy, did you take photograaf of his taatu?'

'Tattoo,' Nitisha corrected.

'Yes, taatu. Did you take photo or not?'

Risha shook her head. 'Not yet.'

Nani tsk-tsked. '*Hazaar baar bola ki don't do taatu, don't do taatu. Lekin aaj kal ke bachey sunte kahaan hain? Taatu karva liya, aur likhvaya kya?* "Desi". What a stupid word!'

'Yes, Nani,' Rishabh agreed. 'Now all he needs to do is have "ghee" tattooed under it and we can sell him at a kirana shop.'

Nani cackled in delight at the fabulous joke. Noticing the ominous glitter in Arjun's eyes, Risha gave Rishabh a discouraging look.

'Arrey, Candy,' Nani continued, 'do take photos of his taatus, *nahi toh vasooli kaise hogi?*'

In an attempt to prevent Rishabh from cracking another tactless joke, Risha turned to Arjun. '*Tattoos?* You have more than one?'

'I didn't realize we're going for full disclosure, Ms Kohli,' Arjun snapped.

Risha was taken aback by his tone. 'Oh-kay.'

Arjun gave her a scathing look. 'I wasn't aware that I need to inform you about *every* tattoo I've ever had.'

What the hell? How could he speak to her like that in front of everyone? She had already put up with his coldness the entire day, and she might be a mere photographer, but she didn't deserve *this*.

Risha tipped her head and gave him a sweet smile. 'Are you sure the tattoo artist didn't forget the needle up your ass?'

Rohan snickered and Rishabh guffawed behind his hand.

Arjun stood up with enough force to tip his chair over. 'We need to talk,' he bit out.

'Or maybe there's *more* than one needle, since there's more than one tattoo?' Risha challenged.

'Get up!' Arjun snapped, grabbing her wrist.

'Bhai!' Nitisha gasped. 'What's wrong with you? Let go of her!'

Risha's face turned red with indignation. Unwilling to make a scene, she stood up, yanked her wrist free and followed Arjun with as much dignity as she could muster.

Nitisha opened her mouth to protest, but Rohan put a hand on her arm and shook his head. For some reason, Nitisha was the only one horrified by Arjun's manners.

Rohan was amused. Rishabh was entertained. And Nani was downright proud.

Risha stood under the peepul tree in silence. Arjun had his back towards her and they'd been standing there for a good five minutes. There was no way Risha would give him the satisfaction of speaking first. Her stomach grumbled in protest and she was tempted to tiptoe away from Arjun to grab a snack. Given that he was staring off into space, it was unlikely that he would notice her absence anyway. At the very least, she could've texted Rishabh to pack some food for the return journey, but she had left her phone on the table. Maybe she could pluck some leaves from the peepul tree and eat those. Were peepul leaves poisonous? She was quite certain they had some Ayurvedic qualities, so they probably weren't lethal. But what if they were unbearably bitter like neem leaves?

Arjun finally turned around to face her. 'I shouldn't have lost my temper like that,' he offered.

Risha stared at the tree obstinately.

'I've had a long day,' he said, raking a hand through his dark hair.

She kept silent.

'My behaviour was inexcusable and I'm very sorry.'

Risha finally looked at him. 'It's okay.'

Arjun seemed a little surprised by that. 'It is?'

'Yes, let's start over.'

'Okay, let's start with why you didn't tell me that you're a journalist.'

'*That's* the reason you've been treating me like crap?'

'Like I said, long day. But in a nutshell, I don't particularly like journalists.'

Risha raised her chin a notch. 'I don't particularly like *you*.'

Arjun almost cracked a smile at that. 'Did you intentionally conceal your profession from me?'

Risha looked at him like he had lost his mind. 'Why would I do that? And if I had to hide the fact that I'm a journalist, why would I tell your sister about it? Also, ever heard of Google?'

Her logic was irrefutable. But her profession wasn't the only thing that was bothering Arjun.

'Do you remember the last time we . . . met?' Arjun asked, carefully studying her expression.

Risha's heart skipped a beat at the mention of their last meeting. The image of him sleeping on the plane flashed before her eyes. Arjun saw her eyes darken and her demeanour soften, and instinctively knew she was thinking about their time on the flight.

He took a step towards her. His face was just inches from hers and her breath quickened in anticipation. 'Risha,' he murmured softly, and she closed her eyes. 'Why didn't you tell me about your boyfriend?'

Risha's eyes flew open and her soft features transformed into an angry scowl. 'Oh, I didn't realize we were going for *full disclosure*, Mr Khanna!'

She turned around and stormed off, leaving Arjun staring after her with a perplexed expression on his face.

He had some nerve treating her like that! He had hoisted her to a shady corner with his entire family watching, and then he had insinuated that she was a liar. And on top of that, he had the gall to ask her about her 'boyfriend' when *he* was the one practically engaged to Priye Ma's niece!

Risha turned to Rishabh and spoke in a grim voice. 'We're leaving. *Now*.' She was relieved when he stood up without another word. She grabbed her camera and backpack and bade the others goodnight.

'Are you sure you don't want to finish your dinner?' Rohan asked politely.

Risha shook her head. 'I'll see you guys tomorrow.'

'Thanks for today, Risha,' Nitisha told her with an apologetic smile before turning to Rishabh. 'Sorry you had to wait so long. It was really nice to meet you.'

Rishabh gave her a dazzling smile. 'No problem, the pleasure was *all* mine.' He bent down to touch Nani's feet and said in flawless Punjabi, 'Thanks for dinner, Nani. I would've loved to stay longer, but I need to take my girl home.'

Nani pulled Rishabh by the collar and whispered something in his ear, causing him to blush like a mischievous schoolboy.

In the car, Risha leaned back on the headrest and looked through her day's work. She had taken a beautiful shot of the peepul tree, lanterns glistening from its branches. Too bad Arjun Khanna had ruined the tree for her, she thought with annoyance.

'What did Nani whisper to you before we left?' she asked Rishabh.

'That she didn't buy for one second that you and I are an item.'

'Thank god! Why the hell were you behaving like we are?' Risha burst out.

'You really don't know?'

Risha raised her hands. 'Know what?'

'The boy is crushing on you, Kohli,' Rishabh said, throwing the car into top gear as they sped down the highway.

'What boy?'

'Arjun Khanna.'

'Are you *insane*? At first he pretended like he didn't know me, then he was inexplicably rude to me, then he—'

'You are so clueless,' he said in disbelief.

'You are so . . . gay!' she said, for lack of a clever retort.

He laughed. 'That's what Nani said to me.'

'Are you serious?'

'Well, she said it in Punjabi. And the words she used were more . . . *colourful.*'

Risha laughed. 'I've never met anyone like Nani, she's hilarious! And she clearly has a great gaydar.'

'Unlike her grandson, who is obviously besotted with you.'

Risha rolled her eyes. 'Sure, because barbaric manners are the way to win a girl's heart.'

Rishabh gave her a look. 'You are *so* naive.'

'Are you and Nidhi in this together? You both keep telling me about random guys who like me, but can either of you explain why I'm twenty-seven years old, single and being driven home by my *gay ex-boyfriend*?'

'I think,' Rishabh conjectured, 'you should've just slept with him on the plane.'

'WHAT?'

'Clearly the sexual tension between the two of you—'

'There is *no* sexual tension!' Risha snapped. And because curiosity got the better of her, she asked, 'Is it even possible to have sex on a plane?'

A mischievous grin crossed Rishabh's face. 'Why don't you ask Arjun Khanna? With a body like that, I can bet he has.'

Great. Now she was thinking about Arjun Khanna having sex.

Rishabh gave her a knowing smile. 'You're visualizing it, aren't you?'

'No, I'm not!' she denied vehemently.

'Doesn't he look like Fawad Khan?'

Risha pressed her knuckles to her forehead. 'I don't want to talk about Arjun Khanna. I have a splitting headache and I'm famished! Let's get kathi rolls from that new place in Vasant Vihar.'

Rishabh wiggled his eyebrows. 'We can always turn around and go to the sushi place.'

Risha leaned her head back and closed her eyes. 'Wake me up when we reach VV.'

Two days to the wedding

For the third time since the morning, Kabir sifted through the photos of Nitisha Khanna's mehndi he had received via WhatsApp. Some of the images had poor resolution, some were overly Instagrammed, but most just lacked readership quotient.

Page 3 was the most-read page of *Delhi Today* and he couldn't print just anything there, especially given that last week, the editor-in-chief, Jay Soman, had pulled him up for a drop in Page 3 likability scores.

Kabir needed better quality images, but he also needed some inside dope, and he needed it fast. He had a good full-length image of the bride, but one image did not a story make. He required a spread, a collage, a goddamn wedding album.

Khudai by Nitisha Khanna had become a major designer label in the last few years, and the going rate for a bridal lehenga was close to ten lakhs, at par with some of the top fashion designers in the country. After Khudai had entered into an exclusive online sales contract with Shopcart.com, the deal had provided Nitisha the marketing fillip she needed, along with a fiancé in the form of Shopcart's founder-CEO, Rohan Singhal.

Last winter, Nitisha had opened a store at DLF Emporio, and around the same time Rohan had raised $1 billion in funding. Theirs was a fairy-tale story, and Kabir was certain the readers would lap it up, especially if he could get a few close-ups of Nitisha's outfits, shots of the family members in intimate settings and some images of the couple with Priye Ma. He was hardly worried about the last category since SoL members had flooded his inbox with those.

Kabir had also heard a rumour that Vikram Walia was attending the wedding, and if that was true, it would make the story highly newsworthy. He could check with Vikram's wife, Nidhi, but no one ever got a peep out of that snooty, secretive bitch. What was the point of being married to a famous person if you never talked about them?

Kabir swiped through the photos and paused briefly at an image of the ghastly Priye Ma. Even the grainy resolution couldn't dull her gaudy make-up.

Maybe he could reach out to the photographer directly and get some photos in exchange for a credit. His source had mentioned the photographer was a girl called Candy. He knew a lot of Delhi-based photographers, but 'Candy' didn't sound familiar. Kabir sent Risha a text message, asking if she knew someone by that name.

At the Shopcart building across town, Risha was busy clicking photos of Rohan and Nitisha. After hearing the story of how they had met, Risha suggested going back to the proverbial 'scene of the crime'.

Two years ago, Khudai had launched a collection exclusively on Shopcart. Shopcart's fashion segment needed the backing of high-end labels like Khudai, and Khudai required the marketing budget to make a mass-media splash. It was a win-win situation, and Rohan and Nitisha had met only twice before signing the deal. The third time, Rohan had asked her to dinner on the pretext of discussing sales and Nitisha had told him to email her instead.

So he'd sent her an email saying, 'I don't really want to discuss revenue. I just want to take you out to dinner. Tonight at 8?' When Nitisha responded with a smiley face, Rohan had sat staring at his screen wondering what that meant.

At 7 p.m., he sent her another email. 'Is that a yes or a no?'

Rohan practically ran out of his office a minute later when Nitisha replied, 'If you have to ask, you're already late.' It was the earliest he had left work since he started the company.

Risha had spent the morning with them at Nitisha's store in south Delhi before heading to Rohan's office in Noida, where they now stood with the Shopcart building gleaming behind them. Risha crouched on the pavement and took a few shots from a lower angle, making them look like the power couple that they were.

When she finally had the shot she wanted, she gave them a thumbs up. 'All done!'

'Phew!' Nitisha exclaimed.

Rohan turned to the dozens of surreptitious eyes that were peeking through blinds on various floors. 'Get back to work or everyone's fired!' he shouted. Laughter rang through the building and Rohan gave his employees a sheepish wave before turning to Risha. 'Can we please get out of here before my hard-ass CEO image is ruined?'

Risha laughed. 'Absolutely!'

As they got into Rohan's SUV, Nitisha turned around to look at Risha, 'Can we interest you in sushi?'

A tiny giggle escaped Risha.

'What happened?' Nitisha asked.

'Rishabh had a major sushi craving yesterday, but I made him get kathi rolls instead,' Risha explained.

Nitisha exchanged a look with Rohan before continuing. 'Rishabh seems like a nice guy.'

'Depends on who you ask,' Risha joked, unzipping her backpack to organize her gear.

'What do you mean?'

'Well, he hardly ever makes a good first impression. Most people don't like him initially, because he's blunt to the point of being tactless. He speaks his mind and doesn't care if he sounds politically incorrect. He's not an easy guy to get along with, but he grows on you,' Risha explained, sliding her camera carefully into its cover.

'But you guys get along fine?'

'We've known each other since we were kids. He's fun to be with and he's always there for me. He's the person I call in the middle of the night when I'm bored or unable to sleep.'

Nitisha turned back to face the road and nodded thoughtfully. 'Hmmm.'

'He's a good guy,' Risha said. 'Did I tell you he just did a shoot for Frontier Bazaar?'

'That's great,' Nitisha answered distractedly.

Rohan shot his fiancée a sideways look before glancing at Risha in the rear-view mirror. 'So can we interest you in kathi rolls instead? I personally prefer them vastly to sushi.'

Risha shook her head. 'Thanks, but I actually have a lunch date with Nidhi. Do you think you can drop me off at Lajpat Nagar on your way?'

'Of course,' Rohan said.

A few minutes later, they pulled up in front of Nidhi and Vikram's sprawling four-storeyed home and Risha asked, 'Are you sure you don't want to come in?'

'No, unfortunately, we need to rush back,' Nitisha said.

'Nidhi will yell at me for letting you leave.'

Nitisha shook her head. 'I have an appointment with the make-up artist, so we're going to grab a quick bite and head back to Gurgaon. Tell Nidhi we said hi and we'll see her tonight.'

Risha nodded, slinging her backpack over one shoulder. 'Thanks for the ride.'

As they drove away, Rohan glanced at Nitisha, concerned by her atypical taciturnity. He knew what was going on in that brain of hers, and since he didn't want to encourage it, he drove in silence.

The previous night, after Risha had left, Arjun returned to the table and kissed Nani goodnight. Nitisha had opened her mouth to unleash a tirade but Arjun gave her a warning look. 'Not now, Chinky.'

She didn't push him, but as soon as Arjun left, she had turned to her fiancé for an explanation.

Rohan briefly explained that Arjun had met Risha on the flight and that his ridiculous prejudice against journalists was the cause of his uncivil behaviour towards her. 'But I think it'll be fine, now that they've talked about it.'

Nitisha had bombarded him with questions but Rohan didn't yield. 'It's not our place, Nitisha. We should stay out of it.'

'If there's anything we can do to sort out their misunderstandings, we absolutely should intervene,' Nitisha persisted.

'No, we absolutely should *not*. Besides, they don't know each other well enough to harbour "misunderstandings". And even if they did, their personal lives are nobody's business but their own. Keep out of it.'

Nitisha had agreed grudgingly, but watching her now, Rohan knew it was still bothering her. With a resigned sigh, he asked, 'What's on your mind?'

'Yesterday, I had the distinct impression that Rishabh is not really into Risha.' Ignoring Rohan's sceptical look, she continued, 'And I'm not sure if Risha is aware of his sexual orientation. She seems fond of him, so maybe she's with him out of loyalty.'

'Nitisha,' Rohan said gently, 'we're getting married in two days. I really don't want to spend this time discussing the sexual orientation of a complete stranger or matchmaking for Arjun. He doesn't appreciate your mother's interference in his life and I'm sure he won't appreciate yours either. So I'm going to say this for the last time: leave him alone.'

Nitisha knew Rohan was right, but something felt amiss. This morning she had barged into Arjun's room as he was getting dressed for work. 'Why are you harassing the photographer?'

Arjun continued working on the knot of his tie and glanced at his sister's reflection in the mirror. 'Good morning to you too.'

'I'm serious, Bhai. She's amazing, and if she quits because of you, I'm going to kill you,' she threatened.

Arjun sighed. 'Chinky, I'm late for work. Can we do this later?'

'No,' she said stubbornly. 'And why are you even going to work? You're hosting a party tonight.'

'I'll be back after lunch. Besides, Tanvi has everything under control,' Arjun said with a reassuring smile.

'You need to apologize to Risha.'

'I already did,' Arjun said tersely.

'What happened to you yesterday? Your behaviour was so out of character, Bhai.'

Arjun gave his tie a final tug and reached for his jacket. 'I said I apologized. Now stop lecturing me, I need to leave for work.'

'Fine. But from now on, if you don't have anything nice to say to Risha, don't talk to her at all.'

Nitisha thought she saw a shadow cross his face, but he nodded before leaving the room.

Risha slipped into Nidhi's dress and gave a little twirl in front of the mirror. The dress looked nice on her, but it felt a little . . . scant. Nidhi was a couple of inches shorter than Risha, but even with flats, the dress showed too much leg.

'Does it fit?' Nidhi yelled from outside the walk-in closet.

Risha opened the door. 'Yes and no.'

'What are you talking about? It's perfect!' Nidhi squealed.

'Well, it's a little shorter than I usually wear,' Risha said, tugging at the hemline of the lime-yellow dress.

'That's because you only wear jeans,' Nidhi said dryly.

'Can you at least give me a jacket or a shrug?' Risha asked, rubbing her arms.

'No.'

Risha pouted. 'Please? I almost froze last night, I can't go sleeveless again!'

'Fine,' Nidhi said, fishing into her closet and coming up with a gold-brocade bolero jacket.

Risha tried it on and stretched her arms to test its snugness. It was super comfortable and the three-quarter sleeves would protect her from the cold. She slid on her gold-and-rhinestone thong sandals and studied her reflection. After seeing Tanvi yesterday, Risha was inspired to put some effort into her appearance. She had raided Nidhi's closet, because, as her friend had correctly pointed out, the Venn diagram depicting Risha's wardrobe and her jeans was basically a circle. She applied some eyeliner and finished her look with a coat of nude lip gloss.

Nidhi gave her an approving nod. 'Now I won't be embarrassed by you.'

Risha rolled her eyes at her friend and reached for her phone, glancing through her unread text messages. One was from her mother mentioning another set of matrimonial ads her father had couriered—did her parents care about nothing other than marrying her off? The other text was from Kabir asking about a photographer called Candy.

Risha froze. How did he know? Was he spying on her? Did he know someone at the wedding? He probably knew all the socialites *and* all the SoLites.

'What's wrong?' Nidhi asked, watching Risha's worried expression.

Risha filled her in quickly. 'There has to be a connection.'

'So what if there is?' Nidhi reasoned. 'You're not doing anything wrong.'

'I never tell him whose wedding I'm shooting, and he never asks. I don't want to mix both worlds,' Risha said. That's a rule she'd been following even before she discovered Arjun's dislike of her 'other world'.

'Tell him you don't know anyone called Candy,' Nidhi said. 'It's the truth.'

'Half-truth,' Risha said uneasily.

'No, it's the whole truth,' Nidhi said firmly. 'Stop being a goody-goody and send him the text.'

Risha nodded and sent Kabir a carefully worded text:

I don't know a photographer named Candy.

Arjun stood at the French windows of his bedroom and took in the panoramic view of the Gurgaon skyline. When he was a kid, his father would take him to the roof of the tallest skyscraper in Gurgaon and ask him to identify all the Khanna buildings. Back then, there weren't as many buildings and there were only a handful of high-rises. Arjun had loved that game, but always resented that they played it in a building that hadn't been constructed by his father.

When Arvind Khanna finally launched Khanna Heights, the tallest residential tower in the national capital region, and asked his son to fly in from New York for the inauguration, Arjun had said no. He'd been working 120 hours a week at the investment bank and was due for a promotion; he couldn't afford to take time off for a trip to India.

Three weeks after the launch of Khanna Heights, Arvind Khanna suffered a massive heart attack. Arjun flew to Delhi immediately, took one look at the terror-stricken faces of Amrita and Nitisha, and made his decision. He resigned a week later, citing personal reasons, and Karan, his friend and roommate, took care of everything in New York.

Over the next two years, Arjun threw himself in his new job as the interim CEO of Khanna Developers. With time, he dissolved the bureaucratic culture of the company by hiring young graduates from top management schools, whom he paid handsome salaries and empowered to take decisions. In turn, they repaid him by committing themselves to the growth of the company as wholeheartedly as Arjun himself.

In addition to human capital, Arjun invested heavily in marketing—revamping Khanna Developers as a young and vibrant brand, instead of a trusted but boring establishment. Watching his son assume his former role with natural ease, Arvind took early retirement, and Arjun took over as the CEO. In the four years since Arjun had joined Khanna Developers, the turnover of the company had more than doubled. Arjun had earned the trust of the board and the shareholders on his own merit, and not just because he was Arvind Khanna's son.

Arjun thought of the two-hour-long meeting he'd had with his leadership team earlier today. They had done the math, and a strike on a plot that size would set them back by millions. Since it was an affordable housing project, there was no way Arjun could pass on the cost to the buyers, and the damages would have to come out of his bottom line. He was tempted to call Yadav and threaten to fire him, but he knew that would only do more harm than good. Not only because it was too expensive to hire a new contractor six months into construction, but also because his father would never let him fire Yadav. Yadav had been their contractor for years, and he was, according to Arvind Khanna, a *'bharosay ka banda'*.

'It's very difficult to find a person you can trust, Arjun,' his father always said. 'And if you find such a person, it is stupidity to lose them over trivial matters.'

Arjun sipped on his Cabernet Sauvignon and turned his attention to the swimming pool. Tonight, he was hosting a party for the couple and fifty of their closest friends and family. They had basically invited everyone under the age of thirty-five who was willing to stay up till the wee hours of the morning, drinking, playing games *and* playing drinking games. Arjun had picked retro video games as the theme of the party, and Tanvi's team had done a brilliant job transforming his penthouse into a full-blown gaming arcade.

His home theatre was connected to a gaming console, and the living room was set up with life-size arcade games like *Pac-Man*, *Space Invaders* and even a pinball machine. Tanvi had recommended upgraded versions of the games but Arjun had vetoed that. 'The whole point of the party,' he explained to Tanvi, 'is to help people revisit the leisure activity of their childhood. It won't work without bad graphics.'

'Purist,' Tanvi had muttered before shouting more instructions into her Bluetooth.

Arjun walked out of his room and was blown away by what he saw. A large Tetris-esque backdrop stood behind the pool with Tetris blocks forming a platform. Guests could choose a foam hat in one of the many Tetris shapes and have a picture clicked on the platform as they walked in. Backlit Ls hung from the trees and Line-shaped benches surrounded Square-shaped tables.

The terrace and barbecue area had been converted into a scene from *Mario*, with tables in the shape of green tunnels, and poufs upholstered like red bricks in place of chairs. The tops of the stirrers looked like toadstools, and Mario-moustache sticks were placed on each table as props for photographs. Tanvi had come highly recommended by Vikram, and she had outdone herself.

Arjun's thoughts drifted to the *other* person Vikram had recommended and he took a long sip of his wine. He was appalled by the way he had treated Risha yesterday. He had not been raised to disrespect a guest in his home, let alone a woman. His actions yesterday were deplorable and, for the life of him, he couldn't understand why he had behaved in such a boorish manner. And even though he had apologized, his apology had felt insufficient, more so because she had accepted it instantly.

He remembered how long he would spend apologizing to Karishma for small things like forgetting to call or rescheduling a date. She used to make him grovel over the phone and forgave him only when he sent her an exotic bouquet of flowers, an expensive bottle of wine or, later in the relationship, a piece of jewellery. So excuse him for being shocked when Risha immediately said, 'It's okay.' Especially given how he had almost manhandled her.

At twenty-nine, Arjun had adequate experience with women. Aside from casual flings, he had dated a few women, even though, besides Karishma, he hadn't let anyone get too close. He maintained his emotional distance, but he was always impeccably polite and unfailingly gentlemanly. So why was his irrational attraction towards Risha causing him to behave like a prepubescent teenager?

The intensity with which he was drawn to her disconcerted him. Of course, she was a beautiful woman, but after watching her the previous day, Arjun had realized his interest in her wasn't just physical. He had been impressed by her photos on the flight, but seeing her in action had taken his breath away.

She was everywhere, and yet she was nowhere to be seen. When he was looking for her just to sneak a glance at her, he could seldom find her. But anytime he thought, 'Wow, that would make a great photograph,' she was right in front, making sure the moment was captured.

She certainly had an instinctive knack for her job, but at the mehndi Arjun had seen glimpses of the warm, funny, friendly Risha he'd met on the flight. Maybe it was a professional tactic, but she seemed to be everybody's favourite person. In all these years, none of his relatives could get along with his mother *and* his grandmother simultaneously, yet Risha had managed to charm both ladies. The elders kept summoning her, the kids kept surrounding her and the men kept showering her with attention.

Too bad she was taken.

Why was she dating that douche Rishabh, anyway? With his hair styled like a model, tightly fitted shirt and perfectly groomed moustache, Rishabh was a typical metrosexual. If Arjun didn't know any better, he would think the dude was gay.

Arjun sank into one of the poufs and saw the patio lights come on. In the distance, he could hear Tanvi giving instructions to the sound guys, and the musical clinking of glasses at the bar.

A woman in a yellow dress walked in through the elevator and Arjun's breath caught in his throat. If her hourglass figure hadn't divulged her identity, the colour of her dress would have.

Arjun remembered Risha telling him on the flight, 'I usually dress in the same colour for the entire wedding, so that it's easy for the bride and groom to spot me—a uniform of sorts. It's subconscious, but after the first day, it works.' Evidently, for this wedding she had picked yellow.

Concealed from her view, Arjun conducted a languid perusal of Risha's appearance. Her soft, brown hair was pulled back in a high ponytail and her black eyeliner brought out the hazel specks in her eyes. Her dress was simple but sophisticated, with a neckline that revealed enough without revealing too much. The thick vertical pleats of the dress tapered down to her mid-thigh, accentuating her curves and showing off her long, long legs.

Before today, Arjun hadn't realized how strong his aversion was to the colour yellow. He hated it with a vengeance. It was the colour of jaundice, of pee, of banana peels on the street. But for some reason, on her it looked . . . tolerable.

Arjun watched her step towards the poolside balcony, stopping for a few moments to admire the view. From his seat on the terrace, Arjun did the same. He observed her in silence for the next few minutes, as she checked the light and took test shots. She changed the lens on her camera and looked up at the Tetris photo booth, rapidly taking shots before glancing back down at the output screen. The action caused her hair to bounce in its ponytail and Arjun wondered how she would look if she wore it down. He admired her sexy, toned legs as she walked the length of the pool, stopping sporadically for photographs. She turned the camera in his direction and gasped in surprise.

Busted.

He gave her a little wave and she waved back before turning away swiftly. He stood up and walked towards the edge of the pool. 'You're early.'

Risha stiffened. 'I'm just here to prep. I didn't realize I was intruding.'

'That's not what I meant.'

'I'm just here to take some test shots, Mr Khanna. I'm sorry if—'

'Arjun.'

She looked confused. 'What?'

'Please call me Arjun.'

'Okay.' She shrugged, turning around.

Arjun's mouth twisted up in a smile. She was one stubborn girl.

'Risha,' he called after her.

She stopped and exhaled. 'Look, I just want to work in peace. If my presence offends you, please take it up with your sister,' she said tartly.

If they weren't separated by the width of the pool, Arjun would've shaken her by the shoulders. 'I really am sorry for the way I treated you yesterday,' he said.

'It's okay.'

'It is?'

'Yes, really. Forget about it.'

Arjun walked around the pool to her side. 'So can we kiss and make up?'

Risha turned to face him, watching the way his blue blazer stretched across his broad shoulders and taut chest, a flash of smooth brown skin peeking from the vee at his neck. Her mouth went dry. 'Huh?'

A smile wafted across Arjun's lips and Risha was certain her knees would buckle under her. 'Can we be friends?'

'Friends,' she croaked.

Arjun cleared his throat. 'How long have you and Rishabh been . . . together?'

Her eyes widened. 'Rishabh is gay.'

'You know that and you're *still* with him?' he asked, horrified.

She burst out laughing.

He frowned. 'What's so funny?'

She shook her head. 'You know, when we first met, I really thought you were normal.' He gave her a baffled look and she continued, 'Rishabh and I have been friends since we were kids. When we were sixteen, we went to watch *Veer Zaara* together. We held hands during the movie, but when we stepped out of the theatre, he said, "I find Veer hotter than Zaara." In doing so, I became the first person he came out to.'

'Oh,' Arjun said stupidly.

'Now, Mr Khanna,' she said with a smug smile, 'may I get back to work?'

And without waiting to hear his response, she spun around and walked away.

Risha stood inside the living room and zoomed in on the photo booth. The guests could not see her as they stepped up on the platform and posed for the event photographer. She adjusted her lens, but just as she was about to click, her screen went pink. She looked up to find Pinku standing in front of her.

'Candyji,' he said with a nervous smile. 'How are you?'

Risha took in his pink satin shirt and shiny aviators atop his gelled hair. His jeans were snug on top, wide at the bottom, and on his pocket, embroidered in sequins, was the word 'swag'. He smelled like he had just showered in Axe deodorant.

'I'm good,' Risha said politely. 'How are you?'

'Very fine. And how are you?'

Risha smothered a laugh. 'I'm good, thanks. And you?'

'Fine.' He smiled at her and looked around nervously. A few seconds passed in silence.

'Did you see the Tetris photo booth?' Risha asked.

Pinku shook his head. 'I didn't went there yet.'

Risha pointed to her camera. 'I was just taking some photos. Would you like to pose for one?'

Pinku nodded eagerly, puffing out his chest. The action exposed a jungle of thick black hair in the gaps between his shirt buttons. Risha had not seen such a hirsute chest since Anil Kapoor in *Tezaab*. She took a step back. 'Why don't you look out at the pool and I'll take your profile?'

Pinku's eyes lit up. 'Facebook profile?'

'Um, no. Your side profile, uh, side *pose*,' she clarified.

Pinku went pink in the face. 'Yes, yes! Side, front, behind, whatever you like, Candyji.'

'You can call me Candy,' Risha said magnanimously.

Pinku's chest expanded further, as though dropping the formal 'ji' made him part of her inner circle. Risha clicked a few pictures, all the while trying to avoid the curly black hair that threatened to burst out of his shiny shirt. Punjabi men, she thought with disgust.

A vision of Arjun's smooth tan chest flashed before her.

Risha shook her head vigorously, trying to make the image disappear.

'You didn't liked it?' Pinku asked, looking crestfallen.

On the contrary, she thought, her mind still on Arjun's sinewy arms and broad shoulders. His decision to go tieless tonight was going to be her undoing. She remembered the adorable look of confusion on his face when she'd told him Rishabh was gay. Despite the five o'clock shadow on his rugged jaw, he had looked oddly boyish. And cute.

'No, it's great,' she told Pinku, briskly snapping more photos.

'Well, well,' said a deep voice behind her. 'If it isn't Auto Rickshaw.'

Only one person called her that.

'Vikram!' she squealed, turning around to give him a hug.

'Like my new hairstyle?' Vikram asked, tilting his head and flashing Risha his famous crooked smile.

Next to her, Pinku blurted, 'Very much! You look very handsome, Walia. I mean Waliaji. Vikramji. Vikram sir. Very handsome, sirji. Just like your new toothpaste ad!'

Vikram turned towards Pinku and held out his hand. 'Vikram Walia, nice to meet you.'

Pinku looked at him with unabashed reverence. 'Arrey, you are so down on earth, sirji. Who doesn't knew you? Myself Pankaj Sabharwal, Nitisha Didi's cousin from Patiala.' And out came the stack of visiting cards.

Vikram took a card politely before turning back to Risha. 'How's it going? Did you—'

'I have played cricket at district level, sirji. I was a fast baller and they used to call me Rawalpindi Express after Shoaib Akhtar. Don't mind, sirji, but India doesn't has too many fast ballers so they had to call me a Pakistani cricketer's pet name.'

Vikram slapped his back affably. 'No worries, man. We should play together sometime.'

'When, sirji?' Pinku asked, his face pinker than ever with excitement. 'I have to went back to Patiala on twentieth, any time before that we can play.'

'Aren't you playing for Nitisha's team tomorrow?' Vikram asked, referring to the cricket match scheduled for the next morning.

'Oh yes, sirji!' Pinku said, looking perilously close to exploding. Then he leaned in and spoke in a clandestine whisper, 'But don't worry, I will try to control my balling speed.'

Not unaccustomed to overzealous fans, Vikram said, 'I appreciate that, man.' Turning to Risha, he said smoothly, 'Do you mind taking a picture of us?'

'Yes, yes, Candyji. I will made it my profile photo,' Pinku said, putting his arm around Vikram, his expression positively worshipful.

Risha gave a little giggle, and Vikram said, 'Hurry up.'

She clicked a picture and feigned a frown. 'I think you guys are not standing close enough.'

Pinku inched closer to Vikram, and Risha took another photo. 'Much better.'

'Thanks,' Vikram said, stepping away.

'Candyji, one from my phone also,' Pankaj said, handing her his phone.

'Of course,' Risha said. 'Why only one? I will take three!'

Vikram gave her a look.

Pinku did a thumbs up in the first photograph, a victory sign in the second and a 'rock on' sign in the third. Vikram looked straight ahead with a practised, but warm, smile on his face. 'Thanks, Pankaj,' he said, and before Pinku could make any further conversation, added, 'I have to go find my wife.'

Pinku nodded and Risha said, 'And I have to take some photos. So I'll see you later.'

'Bye, Candyji. Bye, Vikram Walia sirji. It was pleasure to be meeting you,' he beamed, pronouncing 'pleasure' as 'player'.

Vikram gave him a little wave before turning to Risha. 'You're dead!' He laughed, taking her in a friendly chokehold and dragging her outside.

Risha gasped with laughter, punching him lightly in the stomach, trying to break free of his grip.

'Where's Nidhi?' she asked, as soon as Vikram let her go.

He gave her a hurt look. 'You haven't seen me in weeks and all you care about is Nidhi?'

'How was Australia?' Risha asked, fully aware that he had brought home the Man of the Series award after the five-match tournament.

'It was fine,' he said modestly. 'I missed Nidhi.'

Risha felt a sudden twinge of envy. She loved Nidhi and Vikram dearly, and she'd been genuinely thrilled when they overcame a series of misunderstandings and finally got together. But at that moment, the look of complete contentment in Vikram's eyes made Risha long for something similar.

'Well, she didn't miss you at all,' Risha said, straight-faced. 'She was perfectly happy to spend all her time with me.'

Vikram laughed. 'What do you call the girl version of bromance?'

'Womance,' Risha said, swiftly taking a picture of him laughing.

'What are you guys talking about?' Nidhi said, walking up behind her husband.

'The fact that Delhi is so much better than Mumbai,' Risha said without missing a beat.

'Yes, Vikram, you better agree with that if you want to stay married to me,' Nidhi teased.

Vikram looked at her with unhidden warmth. 'I'll agree to pretty much anything to stay married to you.'

Risha cleared her throat. 'Okay, kids, I've gotta run.' She walked a few feet past them, then turned around and clicked a picture. Vikram had his arms around Nidhi, and he was gazing into her green eyes. Risha looked at her output screen and gave a satisfied nod. Back to work.

Risha stepped out of the restroom and looked around the empty terrace in surprise. Had the party wound up in the sixty seconds she had taken to pee? The dip in temperature had gradually been driving the crowd inside, but at this point there was literally *no* one outside.

Risha heard a muffled cheer from the living room and walked inside. Seated on the couch opposite the TV, their brows furrowed in concentration, were Arjun and Divya.

'What's going on?' Risha whispered to Nidhi.

'They're playing Tetris against each other and it's a pretty high-scoring game,' Nidhi replied.

Lounged on a La-Z-Boy chair, Arjun's friend Angad said, 'First one to 300 has to take a shot.'

A server placed two shot glasses in front of them and stepped aside.

Risha found a good spot a few feet from the TV. Satisfied with her view of the players and the audience, she pointed her camera to the couch and took a picture.

Arjun's gaze flickered to her briefly before returning to the screen. 'You're distracting me.'

'Sorry,' Risha mumbled, taking a couple of steps back.

'300!' the crowd echoed. Divya downed her shot and a waiter replenished her drink.

In contrast to the excited buzz in the room, Angad spoke in a monotone, 'Whoever gets a Line next has to take a shot.'

Divya immediately got a Line and Arjun laughed. 'Burn!'

'The next person to reach a multiple of eleven has to take a shot!' Rohan yelled.

Nitisha gave him a look. 'Nerd.'

'No one is sober enough to calculate, bro,' Angad pointed out.

Without looking away from the screen, Arjun said, 'Candy hasn't been drinking tonight, ask her to do it.'

Great, Risha thought. Arjun and Divya were tied at 310. What number after 310 was a multiple of 11? 333? She had always been bad at math. Not that a roomful of drunk people would notice if she got it wrong.

'It's 333,' Risha said confidently.

Arjun slanted her a lopsided smile, his fingers dancing rapidly on the controller.

'330?' Risha said sceptically.

Arjun looked precariously close to laughter.

'319!' Rohan shouted. 'Divya has to take another shot!'

Divya downed her shot and gasped for breath. Arjun gave her a sympathetic look.

When they reached 400, they were both on the edge of their seats and there was pin-drop silence in the room.

'Is this a world record?' Nitisha whispered.

'The world record,' Angad said in a lackadaisical tone, 'is over a million points.' As the blocks grazed the top of their screens, he added, 'The loser will take a shot.'

Risha saw Arjun slide Divya a sideways glance. The girl could barely keep her eyes open, and it seemed like the only thing keeping her going was adrenaline. Arjun got a Line, and placing it vertically would make four of his rows disappear, giving him a definitive lead over Divya. He placed it horizontally and the audience gasped as the blocks immediately piled on top of each other, ending his game. 'Damn!' Arjun groaned.

Divya screamed and jumped on top of him, practically pinning him to the sofa. She gave him a kiss on the cheek. 'Best day ever!'

Arjun chuckled and gave her a congratulatory hug. 'Good game.' To acknowledge his defeat and appease the crowd, he raised his shot glass and chugged his drink.

Risha stood in the corner and went through the last few pictures of Arjun and his girlfriend. They did look kind of cute together, she thought reluctantly. He obviously cared about her enough to throw the game just to prevent her from drinking too much. Not that he had succeeded, Risha thought wryly, watching Divya jump up and down on the couch like it was a trampoline.

At 3 a.m., there were still a dozen people hanging around and the party was far from over, so Risha didn't feel right going home. Nidhi was tired and Vikram had seemed overly protective of her all evening, so he insisted on taking her home right away.

'Are you sure you'll be okay?' Nidhi asked Risha for the third time.

'Yes! Now please go home,' Risha assured her friends.

She saw Vikram walk up to Rohan and say something. Risha smiled, certain that Vikram was instructing his friend to make sure Risha got home fine. Vikram's concern, while sweet, was unnecessary. Tanvi had designated a car and a driver for Risha, so she did have a way of getting home. She was a tad uneasy about commuting alone with an unknown driver at this hour, but as a worst-case scenario, she could always ask Rishabh to come get her. Him being a night owl paid off at times like this.

An hour later, Risha was reminded of another retro game as she tiptoed carefully across the living room to avoid stepping on the half dozen people passed out on the floor: hopscotch. Most people had left for the night or fallen asleep in one of the rooms, and it seemed like the party had finally wrapped up. Risha was glancing at her watch, ready to call it a night, when she ran straight into a broad, hard chest.

'Ms Kohli.' Arjun smiled, holding her shoulders to steady her.

'Hey,' she said casually, as if his touch hadn't just sent a tingle down her spine.

'Can I get you a drink?' he asked, his hands still on her.

'I'm working,' she said.

'You didn't say no to Nani yesterday,' he pointed out.

'Does *anyone* say no to Nani for *anything*?' Risha asked.

Arjun laughed and took her hand. 'Come on, one drink won't kill you.'

Risha looked down at their interlocked fingers and then up at Arjun. His smile faded and he let go abruptly. Her hand felt cold.

'Okay,' she agreed, more to defuse the sudden tension between them than anything else. 'One drink.'

Something like relief flashed in his eyes, before he gave her an impish grin. 'One Patiala.'

'No way!' Risha laughed, following him to the bar. 'I'll stick to a cocktail, thank you.'

He carried their drinks over to the nearest table and pulled a chair for her. They clinked their glasses and sipped their drinks in silence for a few moments.

'Vikram and Nidhi seem nice,' Arjun said.

Risha's face broke into a wide smile. 'They're the best.'

'How come you didn't leave with them?' Arjun asked.

Risha seemed surprised by his question. 'The party was still on and I didn't want to miss another Tetris face-off.'

Arjun studied her with a glint in his eyes, something that resembled . . . respect? 'Rohan was right about you.'

'What about me?' she asked.

'He said you are sincere. True to your work.'

'He did? That's a nice surprise.'

'Rohan is usually quite stingy with compliments, so, yes, it is. Although I have to say this particular compliment is well deserved.'

Risha looked at him in shock. 'Did you just say something nice to me?'

Arjun laughed. 'Come on! I'm always nice to you.'

She eyed his drink dubiously. 'What is *in* that thing?'

'Ha ha,' he said blandly.

She smiled and sipped her drink. The wind was tossing her ponytail about, and she looked relaxed for the first time that evening. Not that Arjun had been watching her.

Risha admired the glimmering Gurgaon skyline, an asymmetrical crown against the dark night sky. The grandeur of the cityscape was so awe-inspiring that a small sigh escaped her lips. 'The view is gorgeous.'

'Yes, it is,' Arjun said, looking straight at her.

Risha blushed and averted her gaze. Why was he watching her like that? His hot girlfriend was the lead singer of a band and a Tetris pro, he had no business flirting with Risha.

She stood up. 'I'm gonna go.'

He nodded, also standing up. 'I'll drive you home.'

She scoffed. 'No way, you've had too much to drink.'

He gave her a wry look. 'Actually, barring the shot I took three hours ago, this is my first drink.'

'What about the glass of wine you were drinking earlier?' she pointed out.

'Someone's been keeping count,' he teased.

'No, I haven't!' she exclaimed defensively.

'That was like eight hours ago, it doesn't even count. I'm good to drive,' he said.

She shook her head. 'I don't want to trouble you.'

'It's no trouble,' he assured her.

'No, really. I have the driver's number, I'll just—'

'You're not going alone with a driver at this hour,' he stated flatly.

'Fine, then I'll call Rishabh. He's probably up anyway.'

'Rohan asked me to take you home when you're ready, so I'm taking you home,' Arjun said firmly.

Oh. Rohan had asked him.

'Fine,' Risha said nonchalantly. 'I'll get my things.'

'I'll meet you at the elevator in five.'

It was nearly 4.30 a.m. as they hit NH8, en route Risha's home. The early-morning traffic consisted mostly of DTC buses and BPO cabs, so Arjun was driving at an easy pace.

So far, Risha had thwarted Arjun's attempts at conversation with polite monosyllables. He asked if she was feeling cold; Risha said no. He asked if she was enjoying shooting the wedding; she replied yes. He teased her about her 'yellow uniform'; she gave him a cordial smile.

After a few minutes of feeling like a clingy toddler, Arjun gave up and focused on the road instead. When he accelerated to 120 kilometres per hour, Risha grasped the armrest and gritted her teeth. If he thought driving over the speed limit could intimidate her into a conversation, he had another thing coming. She stared out the window in stubborn silence, watching backlit hoardings disappear under flyovers.

Arjun glanced at the backpack resting in Risha's lap. 'Do you carry all your photography equipment in there?'

'Yes.'

'What kind of camera do you use?'

'A Canon 5D.'

'That's a great camera.'

She looked at him in surprise. 'Are you familiar with it?'

Of course he wasn't. 'Of course I am.'

'It was a gift from my parents. I couldn't afford it on my *NT* salary!' she said with such a winsome smile that

Arjun wanted to stop the car in the middle of the road and kiss her senseless.

'That was nice of them,' he said, trying not to think about her soft, full lips.

'They spoil me,' she admitted sheepishly.

I want to spoil you.

The thought had come unbidden to Arjun, and he expelled a breath of annoyed confusion.

'Take a left here,' Risha said, pointing to the gate of her apartment complex. She rolled down the window and nodded to the guard at the entrance, who gave Arjun a suspicious look before releasing the boom barrier.

Arjun parked the car and walked around to open Risha's door, but she was already standing outside the car, holding her hand out formally. 'Goodnight, Mr Khanna,' she said loudly.

Arjun shook her hand with a quizzical look. 'Goodnight, Ms Kohli.'

'Okay, bye,' she said, turning around hurriedly.

'Risha, what's wrong?' he frowned.

The guard walked up to them and handed her a package. 'Thank you, Tyagiji,' she said, clutching it to her chest.

'What's that?' Arjun asked, watching her tight grip on the envelope.

'Spam,' she blurted. Since the package presumably contained more matrimonial ads from her parents, that wasn't exactly a lie.

Tyagiji towered over them with his arms crossed and his eyes narrowed. Arjun returned his stare, unimpressed by the guard's attempt at intimidation and irritated by his nosy attitude. Arjun wanted to talk to Risha and he couldn't do that with this *pehalwan* of a man breathing down his neck.

'Can I come up?' Arjun asked Risha softly.

Tyagiji grunted and Risha rolled her eyes. Arjun turned to the guard with a frosty glare. 'I'm going to walk her to her door.'

Tyagiji stood still for a moment. Then he gave a brief nod and returned to his station.

Risha stared after him, slack-jawed.

In so many years, the man had never allowed Rishabh up to her apartment, let alone any other guy. Even the Shopcart delivery man complained about Tyagiji's unreasonable obstinacy and needless ferocity. And here he was, in the wee hours of the morning, letting a virtual stranger go up to her apartment.

Risha felt a sudden flutter in her stomach. Was she nervous? So what if Arjun was coming up? And so what if he had carried her suitcase and driven her home at night and said they were 'friends'? He had a girlfriend.

He had a girlfriend!

'Risha?'

Risha jumped at the sound of his voice and he watched her curiously. 'Are you sure you're okay?' he asked, striding into the elevator behind her. She swallowed and nodded forcefully. They got off the elevator and he followed her to her door. He watched her fumble with her keys and frowned. 'What's wrong?'

Risha dropped the keys.

Arjun bent down and picked them up. 'Will you please calm down and tell me what's wrong?'

'Nothing,' she said, taking the keys from him.

'I drove you home because I wanted to, not because Rohan asked me to,' Arjun said.

She gave him an indifferent shrug. 'I don't care.'

'Sure you don't,' Arjun said dryly. 'You've been giving me the silent treatment since I mentioned that Rohan asked me to drop you home.'

Oops.

Risha suddenly felt like a petulant child. Arjun had inconvenienced himself by driving her 15 kilometres out of his way at this hour, and she had shown her gratitude by not speaking to him the entire time.

'Thank you for driving me home,' she said sincerely. 'And sorry for acting like a jerk.'

'You're welcome. And it's okay,' Arjun said with an approving smile.

Risha would later tell herself that what she said next was only a courtesy to make up for her earlier rudeness. But the truth was that the sudden dazzle of Arjun's smile had momentarily caused her brain to stop functioning. Before she knew it, she found herself saying, 'Would you like to come in?'

Arjun drew in a sharp breath.

Yes, he thought.

'No,' he said. 'I don't think that's a good idea.'

'Oh,' Risha said, relieved and yet . . . not. Of course, he shouldn't come into her apartment at 5 a.m.; he had a girlfriend. 'Yes, I don't think Divya would approve.'

'Who?'

'Divya Sinha, the rockstar.'

Arjun gave her a puzzled look. 'What's she got to do with it?'

'Everything,' she said stiffly.

'Wait, you don't think Divya and I—*God, no!*'

'But you let her win on purpose!' Risha accused.

He looked abashed. 'You noticed that?'

'Of course. And you guys seemed so . . . close.'

'I just met her *yesterday*,' Arjun said. 'And earlier tonight, I felt bad that she had to take all those shots, so I threw the game. The poor girl was already hammered,' he explained.

Risha gave him an incredulous look. Apparently there was more to Arjun Khanna than a Greek-god-like body and mad Tetris skills.

Risha had a sudden impulse to touch his stubbled jaw. Instead, she said in a sceptical tone, 'But your mom explicitly asked me to take "couple photos" of the two of you.'

Arjun waved away her concern. 'Her lame attempt at matchmaking.'

'Runs in the family, doesn't it?' Risha said dryly.

He chuckled. 'Yes, although Nani is much better at it than Mom is. I do think Harinder, "*pat* name Harry", is quite perfect for you.'

She laughed. 'Maybe I *will* marry him.'

He took her chin between his thumb and index finger. 'Maybe you won't,' he whispered, raising her mouth to his.

'Wait,' she said, taking a step back. 'So why did you say it's not a good idea to come inside?'

'Because you said your parents have a rule against boys inside the house.'

'Oh, right,' she said guiltily.

Arjun broke into the lazy smile she was beginning to recognize all too well. 'But they don't have a rule against boys *outside* the house, do they?'

She shook her head softly, looking up to meet his dark gaze as her pulse leapt in anticipation. He gathered her wrists and pinned her against the door. The light thud of her back against the wood made her giggle. Arjun looked up, a wicked glimmer in his eyes. 'Was that funny?'

She nodded, trying not to laugh.

He placed one hand on the door next to her face and rested the other hand lightly on her hips. Lowering his face to hers, he whispered huskily against her lips, 'How about this?'

Risha gulped and shook her head, her heart beating frantically at his nearness.

He pulled her forward by the waist, standing so close that she could feel the sexy contours of his body against her.

'And this?' he murmured, right before he claimed her mouth in a long, ravenous kiss, igniting each nerve in her body, making her very skin come alive. She parted her lips, inviting his tongue in as he continued to kiss her greedily, passionately.

When he lifted his mouth from hers, she felt torn that their kiss had come to an end. Chuckling at the look of dismay in her eyes, he pressed a long, hot kiss under her earlobe. She arched her neck back and let out a little moan as he left a sizzling trail of kisses from her earlobe to her collarbone.

'Arjun,' she murmured, a tortured whisper of urgent longing.

Ironically, it was the sound of his name on her lips that made Arjun stop. It was the first time she had spoken his name and the sound caused a strange tightening in his chest. He dragged his lips away reluctantly, aware that if he didn't stop now, no goddamn rule and no gentleman's code could keep him from entering her apartment.

He rubbed his thumb across her bottom lip. 'It's been a long night and you have to work in a few hours. You should probably get some rest.'

'You're leaving?' she said, her voice thick with disappointment.

'If I stay any longer, we're probably going to end up breaking a lot of rules,' he said, turning around with visible reluctance.

'Wait!' Risha's urgent tone made him whirl around. She gently raised her hand to his cheek, running her palm over his hard jaw.

His expression softened, as though he was pleased by her voluntary touch. 'What was that for?'

'I've been wanting to do that for some time,' she said shyly.

He turned his face into her palm and kissed it softly. Then he pressed his lips to the back of her hand, the inside of her wrist, trailing kisses up her arm before leaning in for another long kiss.

When they parted a few minutes later, Risha sighed. 'That was nice.'

Arjun laughed. 'Get some sleep, Candy. I'll see you tomorrow.'

'Tomorrow,' she promised, watching him disappear behind the elevator doors.

One day to the wedding

From: Kabir Bose <kabir.bose@newstoday.in>
To: Jay Soman <jay.soman@newstoday.in>
Subject: The F Word

Dear Jay,

I am compelled to write an official complaint about our mutual colleague Sukhdeep Pal Singh Baweja.

Today he called me a 'fucking asshole' in front of my entire team, including two interns. This kind of conduct is unbecoming of a senior editor.

What is most upsetting is that Sukhi and I started our careers together as trainee journalists and have known each other for over half our lives. While I spend close to twelve hours at the office toiling away, Sukhi comes and goes as he pleases. He often shows up to work after 3 p.m., disappears for hours on end and has even been found inebriated on several occasions.

In the past, Sukhi has called me 'elitist bastard' and 'sanctimonious son of a bitch', but using the F word at the workplace is not only derogatory, it is also quite repugnant.

I request you take strict action against him.

Yours sincerely,
Kabir Bose
Editor, *Delhi Today*

From: Jay Soman <jay.soman@newstoday.in>
To: Paloma Chokroborty, EA to Editor-in-Chief <paloma.chokroborty@newstoday.in>
Cc: Kabir Bose <kabir.bose@newstoday.in>
Subject: Re: The F Word

Tuku,

Please inform Prime Minister Modi's office that I need to cancel our appointment for tomorrow. And no, it doesn't matter that it is a *News Today* exclusive.

If need be, please attach a copy of Kabir's mail so that the prime minister can fully comprehend the reason for cancellation. I'm sure he will appreciate that this issue must take paramount precedence over all others.

On an unrelated note, could you please send me last week's reader engagement scores for Sports and *Delhi Today*. I think they stood at 83% and 61% respectively, but I just want to make sure I'm not being a fucking asshole.

J

Nidhi sat down under a large outdoor umbrella, propped her legs up on a chair and sipped her iced tea. Usually, nothing could distract her when Vikram was batting, but today there seemed to be another match going on simultaneously. The groom's side was playing the bride's side in a friendly game of cricket at Rohan's farmhouse. Apparently, it was a tradition in his family since his great-grandfather's time, and looking at the arrangements today, it was fair to say that the Singhals took the tradition quite seriously. Both teams were wearing custom jerseys with team names printed in sports fonts: Super Singhals and Killer Khannas. The Singhals had set up a large electronic scoreboard and even hired a professional umpire to prevent any bias or dispute. But alas, how could a group of Punjabis competing against each other not end up fighting?

The better part of the morning had gone by in a heated argument between both sides. Team Bride argued that having a professional cricketer on their team would give Team Groom an unfair advantage. After an hour of bickering, both teams came to the mutual consensus that it was 'okay' if Vikram, a right-handed batsman, played the match with his left hand.

But even though Vikram was nearing his half-century, Nidhi's attention was diverted by the game her best friend seemed to be playing. This was the second time since the morning that Risha had received a phone call. Risha seldom took calls while working, and almost never smiled stupidly into the phone. Add to that the frequent texting that had punctuated the photography session, and Nidhi was beginning to feel quite suspicious. She feigned a yawn and stretched her arms, leaning in Risha's direction.

'Yes, me too,' Risha said into the phone, followed by a giggle. An actual *giggle*.

Nidhi frowned. *What next? A series of 'no, you hang up first's?*

'Do you want to talk about it?' Risha asked, her tone suddenly serious. 'Okay, let's do that. Yes, I need to get back to work too. I'll see you tonight.'

'I'll see you tonight'?

Risha was shooting the cocktail party this evening, so how could she be seeing anyone tonight? She could be meeting Rishabh after the event, but if the uncharacteristic girlish giggles were any indication, that wasn't Rishabh on the phone. Risha was a thorough professional and there was no way she would sneak out of the party to meet someone. Unless . . . she was meeting someone *at* the party. Someone who was clearly absent from the ongoing cricket match.

'I need to get back to work too,' Risha had said. *Too.*

One person who had given the match a miss due to an 'important work appointment' was Arjun Khanna.

Nidhi's thoughts went to Arjun's party last night. On several occasions, she had spotted him watching Risha. Even as he stood surrounded by a group of friends, nodding interestedly, his eyes had been glued to Risha as she floated around the room, taking pictures.

Nidhi remembered the game of air hockey she had won against Arjun. They had been tied at game point, but the puck had gone whizzing past him at the last moment. Since his gaze was fixated on something behind Nidhi's shoulder, she had turned around to determine the cause of his distraction. Standing behind Nidhi, her camera pointed at their contest, was Risha.

'What?' Risha had asked innocently when Arjun walked off, grumbling to himself. And though Nidhi wasn't certain, it had sounded like he said, 'That dress is too bloody short.'

Smiling to herself, Nidhi called out to her friend. 'Hey, Rish!'

Risha pocketed her phone and swivelled around, a slight flush on her face as she sprinted up to Nidhi. 'What's up?'

'Please tell me you captured Vikram's left-handed six!' Nidhi said, hands flying to her face in the perfect imitation of a paranoid WAG, emerald-green eyes dark with dismay.

Risha's face fell. 'I think I missed it.'

There had been no six. Seven fours, yes. But no six.

'Is everything okay?' Nidhi asked.

'Of course. Why do you ask?'

'You've been on the phone a lot.' Nidhi shrugged.

'Uh, yeah, that was a work thing,' Risha mumbled.

Nidhi cocked her head. '*NT* work or photography work?'

Risha flushed. 'Photography.'

'New client?'

'Something like that,' Risha evaded.

'Let me know if you need help negotiating cost with him,' Nidhi said.

'I think I've got it,' Risha said.

'So it *is* a "him"?' Nidhi asked.

'Um, yes.'

'How did he get your number?'

'From Tanvi.'

'When is he getting married?'

'He's not, his sister is.'

Nidhi hid a smile. Trust Risha to stick to the truth. 'Right. *Tomorrow.*'

Risha looked at her. 'What?'

'Oh, please!' Nidhi burst out. 'You've been talking to Arjun Khanna the entire morning!'

Risha blinked in surprise. 'How did you know?'

'Powers of deduction,' Nidhi said wryly.

Risha filled her in on the events of the previous night—*that* morning—and Nidhi's accusatory look turned excited. 'I'm so glad! Both Vikram and I really like him.'

Risha gave her a big smile.

'Look at you, all adorable and—'

'SIX!' someone shouted in the background.

In a span of a second, Risha turned around, arbitrarily pointed her camera at the pitch and pushed the click button. Nidhi hooted loudly, standing up to clap for her husband. When she peered over Risha's shoulder at the output screen, her mouth hung open in utter shock. Risha had just taken a stunning shot of Vikram watching the ball fly across the boundary, his bat pulled behind him. 'That is plain luck,' Nidhi said in disbelief.

Risha nodded in agreement. She herself wondered how much of her photography was talent and how much was just good fortune.

'Better get to work before my luck runs out.' Risha grinned, jogging in the direction of the boundary, prepared to capture Vikram's half-century.

A few minutes later, Risha watched in amazement as Arvind Khanna ran towards the family chauffeur, Shankar, and enveloped him in a hug. Shankar had just taken Vikram's wicket, and even though Vikram's sixty-three runs had done enough damage, the driver had become Team Bride's hero.

Through her lens, Risha saw the fielding team pile up on Shankar, high-fiving and backslapping him. Shankar beamed with pride when Vikram acknowledged him with a nod before walking off the pitch. One thing Risha could never understand was how, irrespective of their station in life, cricket brought people together. Or how, despite the adulation he received, Vikram managed to stay so grounded.

Risha smiled as Vikram slipped into the chair next to Nidhi and fist-bumped her before bending down to remove his pads. For some reason today, Risha felt just a *tad* less envious of them.

Arjun walked into the grand ballroom of the Oberoi and greeted his grandmother, pressing a chaste kiss to her cheek.

'*Kuch sharam kar,*' Nani said huffily, ignoring his greeting.

Arjun glanced at his watch, mistakenly assuming the reason for her cold response was his fifteen-minute delay. 'It's only 7.45, I'm not that late.'

'All your fault,' Nani grumbled.

Arjun sighed. 'What did I do now?'

'We lost thee match because you diddunt play. *Khanna family ki izzat mitti mein mila di!*' Nani accused.

'Nani, I've never played cricket. Not even in school,' Arjun said, in a fruitless attempt to defend himself.

'Cricket is in your blood. You are Indian, and on top of that, you have Patialvi genes,' Nani said matter-of-factly.

Arjun sincerely hoped she was referring to her own genes and not the maharaja's. Foreseeing the futility of arguing against Nani's infallible logic, he nodded absently.

Nani narrowed her eyes. 'Why are you looking *idhar udhar?*'

Arjun turned to her with a charming smile. 'I'm looking at your beautiful face, Nani. Have I mentioned you look particularly radiant tonight?'

Nani laughed.

'I'm serious.'

'I know. I was laughing at something Candy said earlier,' she explained.

Candy. The reason he had been looking 'idhar udhar'.

'What did she say?' he asked casually.

'She was telling me about thee last wedding she photograafed. Thee whole week thee groom's mausa kept calling her "irritant", and only at thee end of thee wedding did she realize that he meant "radiant".' Nani chuckled, savouring the anecdote.

Arjun smiled. He hadn't heard that one before. Apparently, there was a lot about Risha he didn't know. Like why she followed those primitive rules set by her parents. Or why she looked away every time he gave her a compliment. Or where she was right now.

Arjun glanced around the room quickly, trying to spot her.

'Why diddunt you attend thee match?' Nani persisted.

Arjun had received more bad news this morning. The supplier had confirmed that the sand supplies wouldn't arrive for another three weeks. So even if the strike was called off, the slab-laying work would have to be held off until the raw material arrived. Arjun was beginning to think the bloody property was jinxed.

Reading his pensive look, Nani said, '*Itna kaam mat kiya kar*. Go get yourself a drink.'

Arjun nodded and headed to the bar, thinking that he really did need a drink. Or five. He grabbed a glass of wine and headed back towards Nani's table, but a flash of yellow caught his eye, bringing him to an abrupt halt.

Dressed in a yellow anarkali suit, with a brocade bodice tapering at the waist and gold gota vines dancing on sheer sleeves, was Risha. With her hair tied in a side bun and her dupatta hanging daintily off one shoulder, she was quite the vision in yellow. The colour of sunflowers and yellow sapphires. No, sapphires were hard and Risha was soft. Like butter. Hell, butter was yellow too.

As soon as she spotted him, she walked up to him with a warm smile. 'Mr Khanna.'

'You look stunning,' Arjun said simply.

Risha flushed at the unexpected compliment. Oddly enough, she had been thinking that, dressed in a crisp black three-piece suit, a light stubble on his chiselled jaw, *Arjun* was the one who looked stunning. He looked, in fact, like he belonged on the cover of *GQ*, rather than the business page of *News Today*.

'You don't look so bad yourself,' Risha said, casually raising her camera and snapping a picture.

Arjun lifted an accusing brow and she gave him a guilty smile.

'Have a drink with me,' he said.

'You know I can't. I'm—'

'Working. Yes, I know,' he said impatiently.

'You're distracting me,' she said, repeating his words from the previous night.

'How can I be distracting you already? I just got here.'

Because you've been the only thing on my mind all day.

She took a sudden step back at the unwarranted thought, but recovered with a smile. 'How about I go take some photos of the happy couple's dance performance before your sister fires me?'

'Fine,' he conceded reluctantly. 'But after you're done, I want your undivided attention.'

'What for?' she asked innocently.

Arjun fought the urge to push her up against the wall and answer her question right there. Instead, he said, 'I'm thinking of installing a large frame in my living room and I need your help taking the photograph.'

'Sure, what do you have in mind?' she asked.

'A life-size portrait of Priye Ma.'

Risha burst out laughing and Arjun felt his chest constrict at the sound.

'Decagon of Definitely!' she said with a wink.

He grinned, then leaned his head back against the wall and watched her disappear into the crowd.

Careful, Khanna. Careful.

Risha entered her hotel room, exhausted from the day's events. She placed her camera carefully on the table and changed out of her formal clothes. She'd been hoping to hang out with Arjun, but he had constantly been surrounded by his family. Not wanting to interrupt his quality time with his sister, Risha had quietly slipped out of the ballroom. May as well get some shut-eye, she thought, sliding into her 'Po the panda' pyjamas. She scrubbed off her make-up and brushed her teeth before getting into bed. She was sifting through her Instagram feed, a standard bedtime ritual, when she heard a soft knock on her door. She sat up abruptly, flung aside the covers and darted to the door. She took a deep breath, opened the door and came face-to-face with Pinku.

'Candyji,' he said nervously, 'sorry if I am awaking you.'

His breath smelled like whisky, his speech was slurred and he seemed . . . anxious.

'Is everything okay, Pinku?'

'Pankaj,' he corrected. 'Myself Pankaj Sabharwal.'

Myself going to kick your butt.

'Is everything okay, *Pankaj*?' Risha emphasized.

'Yes, yes, everything is fine,' he said, craning his neck to peek into her room.

Trying her best to keep calm, she asked slowly, 'Then what are you doing here?'

'I, uh, just wanted to ask if you can took my photo with Vikram sir tomorrow? In sherwani?'

Was he kidding? It was 2.30 a.m.!

'I can absolutely *took* it,' she said in a flat tone. 'Now may I go back to bed?'

'Yes, yes. Thank you, Candyji,' he said with a toothy grin.

Risha nodded and shut the door with a soft click. A few minutes later, there was another knock on the door.

'Candyji?' said a muffled voice through the door.

What now? Colour-coordinating his outfit with Vikram?

Risha opened the door with a sigh. 'What is it?'

'Actually I want to talk to you about something important.'

'Can it wait till morning?' Risha asked through gritted teeth.

He hesitated, glancing into her room.

Risha wondered if she could get fired for slamming the door in his face.

'It's about my business, Salwar Hi Salwar.'

'You want me to take pictures?' she guessed.

Pinku nodded emphatically, seeming relieved.

'Why don't we discuss it later?' Risha evaded.

He gave her a happy smile. 'Are you *shaadi-shuda*?'

That was the last straw. 'Goodnight, Pinku.'

He opened his mouth to correct her. 'Myself—'

But Risha had already shut the door.

She was nearly asleep a few minutes later when she heard another knock on her door. She groaned and buried her head under her pillow. Maybe if she pretended to be asleep, he would go away.

There was another knock, this time louder.

With the last shred of professional courtesy she had left in her body, Risha dragged herself out of bed, purposefully knotting her hair in a bun and clenching her fists at her side. Bride's cousin or not, Risha was going to give this guy a piece of her mind. 'It's 3 a.m., Pankaj!' she yelled, opening the door.

Except the person at the door wasn't Pankaj.

'Already forgotten my name?' Arjun said, the corners of his mouth lifting in a teasing smile.

'Oh, hi.' Risha jerked back in surprise, and the movement sent her hair tumbling down her shoulders in long, flowing waves.

Arjun jolted back in shock. 'Shit,' he whispered, his mouth agape.

'What?'

'Your hair,' he rasped.

'I know,' Risha said with a helpless smile, raking her fingers through her hair, trying to straighten it. 'It's a mess.'

'No, I just meant that it's . . . *longer* than I expected,' he explained, his awestruck gaze still riveted on her hair.

Risha suddenly felt very self-conscious. And very awake.

'Uh, yeah, it's pretty long,' she said, feigning a casual yawn.

'Do you want to go back to sleep?' he asked gently.

'No!' she exclaimed.

Arjun smiled and took her hand. 'Then come with me.'

'But I'm in my pyjamas,' she protested, grabbing her phone and key card before he pulled her into the corridor.

'You're fine,' he said, walking to a room diagonally across the hall.

'Whose room is this?' Risha asked.

'Mine.'

'Oh,' she said, following him inside. 'Isn't the immediate family staying on another floor?' she wondered out loud.

Arjun slid off his jacket and hung it on a chair. 'They are, but I traded rooms with one of my cousins.'

'I see,' Risha said, watching Arjun yank off his tie and toss it on a chair. Still wearing the waistcoat of his three-piece suit, he rolled up his sleeves, and the movement sent a delicious ripple up his biceps.

Is he going to take off the waistcoat next?

Risha absently twisted a strand of hair around her finger.

And his shirt after that?

She wrung her hands in her lap.

What if his pants follow?

Panic rose in her throat.

And then—

'Risha?'

She jumped at the sound of his voice.

Arjun scanned her face worriedly, it was white as a sheet. Which is why, even though it wasn't the *whole* truth, he said softly, 'I just want to talk, okay?'

She nodded.

'Would you like to sit?' he asked, then frowned as she sat down stiffly on the sofa in the far corner of the room.

The Risha he knew was independent and self-assured, ever ready with a jibe or a quip. The Risha he knew was *not* scared or anxious. And she certainly wasn't the type to back away into a corner.

Arjun took a seat next to her, carefully leaving some distance between them. Observing her rigid posture, he asked, 'Do you want to tell me what's bothering you?'

What's bothering me is that you're the most handsome man I've seen in my life. What's bothering me is that you're kind and chivalrous and funny. What's bothering me is the deep concern etched on your face right now. What's bothering me is that you've probably had sex on a plane!

'I'm not very good at this,' Risha said, gesturing to the space between them.

Arjun seriously doubted that, but he gave her an understanding nod and waited for her to continue.

'I'm . . . I'm a little nervous,' she admitted.

Arjun felt an involuntary stab of emotion. She looked so frightened, so fragile, that he desperately wanted to take her in his arms and comfort her. But he sensed that would only make her more anxious, so he gave her a reassuring smile instead. 'I just want to spend time with you, that's all.'

'Me too,' she said softly.

Arjun brought up a topic he knew would help calm her down. 'I hear the match today was a real cliffhanger?'

Risha scoffed. 'If you call losing by thirty runs a cliffhanger!'

'Did you get some good pictures?'

Suddenly her entire body relaxed and she animatedly shared details of her day. Arjun watched the way her eyes lit up and the myriad emotions that played across her face as she described the cricket match.

'It's weird how on a cricket field, they were all equals,' she said in amazement.

He chuckled at her enthusiasm. 'Maybe you should diversify into sports photography.'

'Maybe I will,' she said.

'Is that something you would seriously consider?' he asked.

'I don't know, maybe someday. Right now, I'm happy with just wedding photography.'

She hesitated.

'Go on,' Arjun prompted.

'To be honest, handling two jobs simultaneously is too much. Sometimes I don't get sleep for days.'

'Tell me about it,' he muttered under his breath.

'What?' she asked.

'Just wondering why you don't do photography full-time. You're clearly very passionate about it, and it seems to make you happy,' he said.

'If it takes off, I'll do it full-time,' she said.

'If you do it full-time, it will take off,' he challenged.

'You don't know that.'

'You're obviously very good at what you do. But you need to put yourself out there completely, hold nothing back. Not having a safety net is often what keeps you from falling.'

Something clenched inside her chest and she tried to come up with a witty rejoinder to change the subject, but she couldn't.

Arjun gave her a long, scrutinizing look.

Wary of the way he was watching her, she blurted, 'I'm hungry.'

His gaze drifted to her lips and he whispered, 'So am I.'

Risha snatched up the room-service menu from the table in front of her and started flipping through it voraciously. Arjun chuckled and stood up, picking up the phone on the nightstand. 'What would you like to eat?'

'The primal chocolate ganache tart,' she said, her eyes bright with anticipation.

Of course, he thought with a smile. He repeated her order into the phone, then as an afterthought, added, 'Actually, make it two.'

She looked at him in surprise. 'I thought you didn't like chocolate.'

He slid back into the couch next to her. 'On the contrary, I love chocolate.'

'But on the flight you traded your chocolate torte for my mango cheesecake,' she said, furrowing her brows.

Arjun gave her a wolfish grin.

Realization dawned on her face. 'Oh.'

Dressed in her *Kung Fu Panda* pyjamas, with her long hair tousled and a gorgeous blush creeping up her cheeks, Arjun thought Risha was more beautiful than any woman he had ever seen.

His eyes darkened and his voice dropped to a husky whisper. 'And in the interest of full disclosure, I think you should know where the other tattoo is.'

She peeked at him from lowered lashes. 'It's only fair.'

Arjun saw the soft invitation in her eyes and leaned in with such purpose that it made her breath catch in anticipation.

But the kiss that followed surprised her—it was gentle, tender, deliberate. He brushed his lips against hers ever so lightly, taking his time. His hands drifted up and down her arms in a gesture that was both sensual and soothing. Warmth coursed through Risha's veins as she realized what Arjun was doing. He was easing her into the kiss, inviting her to set the pace, letting her hold the reins.

Risha slid her hands up his muscular chest. The unbridled hammering of his heart under her palms made Risha positively giddy with power. But the feeling of being in charge didn't last long, because as her hands made their way up his broad shoulders, Arjun's soft, teasing kiss became heated, possessive, demanding.

With a muffled groan, he yanked her on to his lap and roughly tangled his hands in her hair. The stormy intensity of his mouth against hers sent a jolt of electricity down her spine, and Risha kissed him back, matching his passion with every fibre of her being, wrapping her arms around his neck, moulding her body to his. And that was all the encouragement Arjun needed.

He slipped one hand under her shirt, caressing her back, tracing the curve of her waist, tenderly running his fingertips against her flat stomach. His hand inched upwards and suddenly Risha gasped, jerking back.

'What's wrong?' he asked, pulling himself out of a stupor.

'There's someone at the door,' she whispered, wriggling off his lap.

That's when he heard the knock.

Bloody room service.

Arjun stood up reluctantly. 'I'll get it.' Then he sat back down and said meaningfully, 'Actually, I think it's better if *you* get it.'

Risha leapt off the sofa and fanned her face fervently, letting the server in.

A few minutes later they sat cross-legged on the bed, devouring the remnants of their desserts. 'Are you sure you're not sleepy?' Arjun asked, popping the garnish strawberry into his mouth.

'Not really. You?'

'I don't . . . I'm not.'

She cocked her head. 'You don't what?'

'I don't sleep much,' he confessed.

'Why?'

'I just have a lot on my mind. Work-related stuff,' he said evasively.

'Earlier today on the phone, you said you were having a bad day. What was that about?'

Arjun hesitated, tempted to make a joke about it. Something along the lines of 'I missed Vikram Walia's half-century, of course it was a bad day!' But for some reason he didn't feel like lying to Risha. So he poured out the entire story about the ongoing strike, its cost implications and the creeping deadline. He vented for nearly half an hour and Risha listened intently without interrupting. When he finished speaking, she didn't say anything for a few moments.

'Too much information?' he asked.

'Not at all. But I do have a few questions.'

'Shoot.'

'How did you end up working at Khanna Developers?'

'Dad had a heart attack, so I decided to leave my job and move back home.'

'Did you resent that?' she asked bluntly.

'Maybe in the beginning, but not any more,' he said honestly. 'I actually really love my job. It's just a bit overwhelming at times because I'm unable to disconnect from work.'

This was more than Arjun had shared with Ali on their boys' trip. He shifted uncomfortably, but Risha gave him an understanding nod.

'Are strikes in the private sector a common thing? I mean, I've never heard of anything like this.'

'They're fairly uncommon, but not unheard of. Most companies work really hard at keeping labour strikes under wraps because it makes for bad PR.'

'Do you think there's more to the story than just rates?' Risha asked.

Arjun thought about that. 'Not to my knowledge.'

'I think there could be,' she said tentatively. 'I don't know much about the real estate sector, and I have no experience dealing with unions, but I think sometimes people just want to feel like . . . people. They don't want to hear about project delays and dents in the bottom line. They want to feel like they are more than just cogs in the wheel. They want to believe that, in the larger scheme of things, they matter.' She paused, feeling a bit silly. 'I don't know if that makes sense.'

Arjun shook his head. 'Actually, that makes a lot of sense. It's just that I'm better with numbers than I am with people. Ever since I've taken over, I haven't been able to invest time in labour relations. That was Dad's forte.'

'Maybe the contractor and his team find you . . .' Risha paused, looking for the right word.

'Unapproachable?' he suggested.

'It's possible,' she said.

'It's probable,' he admitted reluctantly. 'I got similar feedback from my PR team about the press. Journalists just don't seem to like me,' Arjun said, as he gathered their empty plates and set them on his nightstand.

'Not *all* journalists,' she pointed out.

His face broke into a boyish smile at her implication. 'Well, you're unlike any journalist I've ever met.'

Hell, she was unlike any girl he'd ever met.

'I get that a lot.' She smirked.

'By the way,' he said randomly, 'did I see you punch your number into that blond flight attendant's phone?'

Risha looked surprised. 'You don't miss anything, do you?'

'Why *did* you give him your number?'

She gave him a guilty look. 'He only agreed to upgrade me in exchange for my phone number.'

'That son of a bitch!' Arjun bit out furiously. 'What the hell was his name? I'm going to call the airline's CEO and—'

'Chill! It's not like I gave him my real number.'

'You're kidding.'

Risha snorted. 'You think I just give out my real number to every guy who asks for it?'

'That depends on how often guys ask for your number,' Arjun said dryly.

'Every now and then,' Risha shrugged. 'Mostly at weddings.'

'Has it happened at *this* wedding?'

Risha saw the possessive glint in his eye and gave him an irrepressible smile.

'*Has* it?' Arjun demanded.

Three times, actually. But Risha didn't want to dampen the mood, and since she did not advocate lying, she went with evasion instead. 'Guys who really want my number don't ask *me* for it.'

Arjun saw through her attempt to change the subject, but humoured her nevertheless. 'Really? Who do they ask?'

'The wedding planner,' Risha teased, since that was how Arjun had procured her number. She pulled up the blanket over their legs and slid closer to Arjun. Where her teasing didn't distract him, her nearness did.

'I guess the fake phone number exchange was worth it,' Arjun murmured, lacing his fingers with hers.

'Why's that?' Risha asked, resting her head on his shoulder.

'Because if you hadn't been upgraded to business class, you wouldn't have met me.' He smirked.

'I would've met you at the wedding,' she pointed out.

'Yes, but then I would be just another guy at a wedding.'

'Not true,' she said.

'No?'

She gave him a disarming smile. 'No, you would be just another guy at a wedding, *but* with a lame tattoo.'

Arjun laughed and tugged her ear playfully. 'Brat.'

Risha raised her head from his shoulder and looked at him. 'Can I ask you something?'

'Sure,' he said, a little perturbed by how his shoulder suddenly felt . . . bereft.

'How did you convince Bitchi—uh, Kritika on the flight to let me stay in my seat?'

'I told her she can't downgrade an upgraded passenger,' he said, yearning for the feel of her cheek on his shoulder.

'That's it?'

He grinned at her sceptical look. 'Broadly.'

'Then why didn't she come back to business class for the rest of the flight?' Risha asked suspiciously.

'Because,' Arjun said, firmly tucking her head into the crook between his neck and shoulder, 'I can be very persuasive when I want something.'

'Brat,' Risha muttered.

Arjun chuckled into her hair. Her long, brown waves grazed his arm and he took a strand between his fingers. It was soft, just like the rest of her. He sat there in comfortable silence, breathing in her citrus scent and playing with her hair for a long time, until the weight on his shoulder got heavy. Contrary to her claim, Risha had obviously been quite sleepy.

He gently moved her beneath the covers and placed a pillow under her head. Her long hair adorned the pillow in careless disarray and her thick lashes rested softly on her cheeks. She looked so vulnerable as she slept, with nothing to hide behind—no camera and no snarky remarks. Arjun felt a strange surge of protectiveness tide over him as he tucked her in.

The gentlemanly thing would be to go sleep in her room, or at least move to the couch. Arjun laid down next to her and closed his eyes.

He could postpone being a gentleman for one night.

The Wedding Day

Risha awoke the next morning with the soft buzzing of her cell phone alarm. She stretched her arm to the nightstand and turned it off.

The first event this morning was the choora ceremony. The bride's maternal family would perform a short ritual and make Nitisha wear the traditional red and ivory bridal bangles. The wedding was an afternoon affair and Risha wanted to get some extra time at the venue before the guests started meandering in.

Risha tried getting out of bed but was held back by something. She looked down to see Arjun's arm wrapped around her waist. Unconsciously, his grip tightened in his sleep and Risha smiled to herself. She gently lifted his arm and, not wanting to wake him up, tiptoed out of his room.

Inside her own room, Risha fished out the day's outfit from her overnight bag—a yellow churidar and silk kurta with a silver border stitched on to an uneven hemline. She removed the camera charger from the socket and plugged in her phone charger instead. The memory card of her camera was placed neatly on the table next to her camera and the rest of her photography gear. She felt a twinge of uneasiness because she couldn't remember taking the memory card out of her camera last night. But then last night seemed so long ago that perhaps it had just slipped her mind.

A few minutes later, showered and dressed, Risha stood in front of the mirror wondering what to do with her hair. She pulled it up in a banana clip, then remembering how Arjun had watched her hair last night, wore it down instead.

'Dahling, now do Divya!' Amrita squealed in excitement.

'No thanks, Amy Aunty. I think I'll pass.' Divya grimaced.

'I insist! You're the only one left,' Amrita said.

Seated on the large sofa of the bridal suite, Nitisha turned to Divya with a polite smile and gestured for her to come squat next to the sofa.

As per custom, the bride would shake her hands over the head of each single girl. If a metallic *kaleera* from her wrist fell on the bachelorette's head, the latter would be married within a year.

Divya sat on the floor next to Nitisha, looking quite blasé about the whole thing. Amrita Khanna clapped her hands. 'Come on, Divya!' Then she gave Nitisha a wink.

Apparently, Amrita was quite set on making Divya her daughter-in-law within the year, Risha thought wryly from her position on the floor opposite the couch.

After a few seconds, when no kaleera fell atop Divya's head, Nitisha withdrew her hands and the crowd, consisting mostly of SoL aunties, groaned, 'Oho!'

Amrita's shoulders sagged.

'What did I miss?' a deep voice asked.

Risha turned around and saw Arjun stride into the suite.

If Risha was writing an article for *Delhi Today*, the word she would use to describe the colour of Arjun's kurta would be 'jonquil'. Or 'amber'. Or even 'mustard'.

But at that moment, the thought that crossed her mind was that his kurta was, unequivocally, *yellow*.

'Bhai!' Nitisha exclaimed. 'Where have you been?'

'I . . . *overslept*,' Arjun said cautiously, as though doubting the accuracy of his own words.

Nitisha's astonishment mirrored her brother's. 'Wow.'

'I know,' he said, still trying to digest this unprecedented occurrence.

'We just finished with all the girls,' Nitisha explained.

Seated on a tall wingback chair, looking very much like a queen on a throne, Nani's voice boomed with authority. 'Not all.'

'Yes, all,' Amrita said with certainty.

'Not *all*,' Nani repeated.

Nitisha looked puzzled. 'Whom did we miss, Nani?'

'Candy.'

Risha groaned inwardly. Maybe if she remained silent, they would assume she'd left.

Amrita laughed, as though the notion of including Risha in the ceremony was positively ludicrous. 'But she's the *photographer*!'

Risha was tempted to hide under the coffee table.

'She is photograafer, but she is also *bech*elor,' Nani said.

'Single,' Nitisha corrected.

'Crect,' Nani agreed. 'Single *bech*elor.'

Perhaps, Risha thought, she could crawl out the door unnoticed.

'Yes, where is Candy?' Arjun asked, looking straight at her, his tone dripping with amusement.

Risha threw him a dirty look.

'*Are* you single?' Arjun smirked, his question laden with meaning.

Risha stood up, handed her camera to Nani and tossed back her long hair. 'Let's do this.'

Risha crouched on the floor next to Nitisha, and Arjun gave her a smug smile. *You didn't say yes.*

She glowered at him. *I didn't say no either.*

Nani watched the exchange between them with a secret smile.

Arjun kneeled on the floor next to Nani's chair and pointed the camera up at Risha. Nani leaned down and whispered to him, 'You both are a match.'

Arjun cocked his head. 'Because we're wearing yellow?'

'That also.' Nani nodded.

Arjun opened his mouth to ask what she meant by that, but was distracted by the sound of laughter. Chinky's head was bent down conspiratorially as she whispered something to Risha. Risha broke into peals of laughter, and a few thick strands of hair framed her face as she shook her head.

Watching the moment between the two women, Arjun felt a strong tug of emotion. The feeling was raw and unfamiliar, but so potent that it shook him up completely. So much so that he lost his balance and fell on his butt. That drew another laugh from Risha, which kind of made it worth it. He gave her a quick wink and mouthed 'good luck', but she just rolled her eyes at him.

Nitisha raised her hands above Risha's head and shook her hands vigorously, causing a storm of kaleeras to go crashing into each other. As she yanked her wrists apart to untangle the kaleeras, a chunky piece of metal fell on Risha's head with a loud thud.

'Ow!' Risha winced, rubbing her head just as the rest of the congregation chorused, 'Awww!'

Risha turned to Arjun with a challenging look. *Bring it on, buddy. Let's get the teasing remark or sarcastic comment over with.* But there was none.

Instead of an amused smile, Arjun was watching her with a strange expression on his face.

'Very good!' Nani chimed, breaking their eye contact.

Nitisha shot her brother a knowing smile and he stood up abruptly, handing Risha her camera. 'I hope the pictures came out fine,' he said, looking inexplicably uneasy.

Risha glimpsed through the last few images and nodded, but when she looked up from the camera, Arjun was nowhere to be seen.

'Candy, you must save thee kaleera till thee time you get engaged,' Nani said in a grave tone. 'And when you get engaged, you must leave thee kaleera at a gurdwara immijately.'

'No, you are supposed to leave it under a peepul tree,' said Nitisha's chachi.

'No, no, it's a neem tree,' her masi contradicted.

'Don't listen to them,' Nani said dismissively. 'You have to leave it at a gurdwara.'

'Yes, Nani,' Risha replied distractedly, wondering where Arjun had disappeared.

Arjun spent the next hour at the gym. There was some time to kill before the wedding ceremony, because, thanks to Tanvi, everything was working like a well-oiled machine. He had missed his morning run because he had—he still couldn't believe it—slept through his alarm. But that wasn't the only reason he was running himself into the ground.

After watching his sister and Risha this morning, a strange lump had formed itself in Arjun's throat. The two women really seemed to be getting along. Although, now that he thought about it, there was hardly anyone Risha *didn't* get along with. But watching Chinky and Risha share a private moment had painted such a strong picture in his head that it had thrown Arjun off his game. So far he had been living in the moment, enjoying his time with Risha. But the way he had felt this morning was unlike anything he had ever felt before. And it terrified him.

The previous night, Arjun had thought Risha was more stunning than any woman he'd ever met. But it wasn't just the sexy figure she hid behind her pyjamas that he found so irresistible. It was her innocent charm and warm humour that made Arjun's heart clench inside his chest.

It had taken him every shred of restraint in his body to stop at just kissing her. He remembered how nervous she'd seemed at first, but the moment his lips had touched hers, she'd clung to him like she couldn't let go. She seemed to enjoy spending time with him and kissing him, but she hadn't actually *told* him that this was anything more than a weekend flirtation. And yet, last night, when she fell asleep on his shoulder, something had stirred inside him. He had felt like she wanted to be close to him, that she even trusted him.

Arjun had never been so diverted by a woman in his life. For the first time in years, he woke up thinking not about work, but about Risha. He wanted to look at her, touch her, talk to her, make her laugh. He just couldn't get enough of her.

So he ran faster.

'Are you trying to break the treadmill?' a voice called out.

Arjun turned his head and saw Vikram Walia doing leg presses a few feet behind him.

They had been introduced on game night and, in spite of his celebrity status, Walia was a friendly, laid-back sort of guy.

Arjun grinned. 'Hey, man. Just overcompensating for missing my morning run.'

'Don't wear yourself out, you have a wedding to attend,' Walia pointed out.

'True.' Arjun reduced the speed on the treadmill and eventually shut off the machine. He grabbed a towel and wiped his neck, walking towards Walia. 'How's it going?'

'Great. I just hope I don't get kicked off the team because I ate too much at Singhal's wedding,' the cricketer grinned, patting his perfectly flat stomach.

Remembering the well-publicized episode two years ago when Walia *had* been kicked off the team, though not for being out of shape, Arjun chuckled. 'You could always ask Rohan to compensate you.'

'Like that would ever happen,' Walia joked.

Arjun laughed. 'When do you fly to Sri Lanka?'

'In a couple of weeks,' Walia responded.

'What do you plan to do with your free time?' Arjun asked, taking a long sip of water.

'Give several interviews to the sports desk at *News Today*,' Walia said dryly.

'How come?'

'It's just an excuse to see Nidhi at work. I go say hi to the sports editor and then drag Nidhi out to lunch. Everybody wins.' He grinned, his expression softening at the mention of Nidhi.

The man was obviously very much in love with his wife. The lump in Arjun's throat grew bigger and he tried to wash it down with the rest of his water.

'It was good seeing you, man,' Arjun said. 'We should catch up while you're here.'

'I'm sure the girls will see to it,' Walia said.

Arjun raised a brow. 'The girls?'

'Nidhi and Risha,' Walia replied casually.

So Risha had been talking to her friends about him. Interesting.

'Can't wait,' Arjun said, walking out of the gym with a big grin on his face.

The wedding was beautiful. The mandap had been set up in the large garden of the hotel and its modern glass facade made a picturesque background for the ceremony. The theme for the decor was marigolds—a curtain of the orange flowers hung over the mandap, long strings were suspended from the shisham trees that flanked the garden, and tea lights on a bed of marigolds served as the centrepiece for each table.

The newly married couple sat at a table for two, eating a late lunch. Unlike the huge family supper that typically followed Indian weddings, Tanvi had planned an intimate meal for Rohan and Nitisha to enjoy their first few moments as husband and wife.

After being on her feet for six hours non-stop, Risha finally found a quiet corner under a tree and sat down, exhausted. She leaned against the trunk and folded up her legs, resting her chin on her knees. She spent several minutes flipping through the images, mentally critiquing each one along the way.

A photograph of Nitisha stepping on to the sun-dappled mandap.

Rohan winking at Nitisha—a moment no one saw—following Panditji's interpretation of the holy decree of 'preserving wealth': that Nitisha ought to use her credit cards only with permission from Rohan.

Nitisha rolling her eyes immediately after that—a moment everyone saw and laughed at heartily.

Arjun hugging his sister after the ceremony, his lips pressed to her forehead. Risha paused at that photograph and her heart gave a little lurch.

'Hey.'

Risha looked up and saw Arjun standing in front of her, looking dapper in a grey linen *bandhgala*. The man seriously looked less like a CEO and more like a model.

'What are you looking at so intently?' he asked, craning his neck to catch a glimpse of her screen.

'Nothing!' she said, hastily pressing the camera screen into her knees.

He crouched down next to her and handed her a plate. 'I thought you could use this.'

Risha looked at the plate and then back at Arjun. Her face filled with awe as she plucked the dessert plate from his hand and whispered reverently, 'You are a god.'

Arjun laughed, fully expecting that reaction. He pressed his back into the tree trunk and sat next to her in silence as she gorged on the chocolate cappuccino cheesecake. After a few minutes, Risha found Arjun looking at her expectantly. Had he asked her a question?

'What?' she asked.

'I asked if you're sticking around for a bit.'

'What for?'

'I'm accompanying Chinky to her new home and I'll be back in a couple of hours. Will you still be here?' he asked.

'Well, I wanted to get in a few hours of post-processing today since I go back to work tomorrow,' she said, licking the back of her spoon. 'So I think I'll head home after the vidaai.'

Arjun nodded. 'Of course.' He took out a handkerchief from his pocket and wiped the corner of her mouth.

Oh god, did she have chocolate on her face again? Why couldn't she just eat like a grown-up? Risha reached for her phone, turned on the selfie camera and scrubbed the sticky chocolate off her face.

Arjun took the phone from her, tilted his head just so it was grazing hers and took a selfie.

Handing her phone back, he asked softly, 'Can I take you to dinner tomorrow?'

'I'd like that.'

'Last one,' Nani said.

Arjun looked at the blurry figure in front of him and slurred, 'I can't.'

He had spent the last few hours getting sloshed with Nani and Angad. To be fair, only Arjun and Angad were drunk. Nani looked like she had been sipping on nimbu pani the entire night.

'I am leaving for Patiala tomorrow. And thee next time you see me I will be lying flat on a funeral pyre,' Nani said.

Why did old people always use that scenario to get their way?

'You've been saying that for the last ten years, Nani,' Arjun said dryly.

Nani ignored him and turned to his friend. 'Angad, refill.'

Angad swayed his way to the bar, knocking over a small wooden stool and sending it crashing to its fate.

Arjun looked blankly in the direction of the noise. 'That was loud.'

'Nani,' Angad called out to her, 'I will drop you to Patiala on my way to Ludhiana. It's on my way, Nani, on my way.'

Nani shook her head. 'No, I will go by train. It is thee most best way to travel.'

'Just "best",' Arjun said.

'Crect,' Nani agreed. 'Just most best.'

'But driving is more better,' Angad slurred, handing Arjun his drink.

'I have to work tomorrow, Nani,' Arjun groaned, reluctantly taking the glass from Angad and accidentally sloshing some whisky on the table.

'Why you *jawaan* people are always saying that? I have to work, I have to work. You have to relax,' Nani said.

'Patiala is on my way, Nani,' Angad reminded her, looking ready to pass out.

'I need to fix the strike,' Arjun mumbled.

'You need to fix your *life*,' Nani retorted.

If he hadn't consumed an illegal amount of alcohol, Arjun would have given a facetious response. But he was in no mood for levity, so he nodded in agreement. 'I do.'

'And I think you know how,' Nani said.

Arjun lifted a brow in inquiry.

'Onmyway,' Angad mumbled, half asleep.

Arjun's phone beeped and he reached for it. A photo popped up on his screen—the selfie he had taken with Risha that afternoon. Arjun chuckled at the caption she had given it: 'Pretty girl with average-looking boy'. His expression in the photo took him by surprise—he looked . . . *happy*.

'That's how,' Nani said, tipping her head in the direction of his phone.

Arjun narrowed his eyes, partly to gauge her meaning, but mostly so he could focus on her. After a brief staredown, Arjun finally looked away.

'She is good for you,' Nani said.

Arjun remained silent.

'And if you don't snatch her up,' Nani went on, 'that idiot Pinku will.'

Arjun was astounded. '*Pinku*? As in Pinku Sabharbaal?'

Nani ignored the rude, albeit accurate, sobriquet. 'Crect. Pinku will marry her, and your mother will continue to parade *hazaaron* circus girls in front of you, until one fine day Priye Ma will become your mother-in-law.'

The thought almost made his alcohol come back up.

Arjun took a deep breath. Never in his wildest dreams had he imagined saying these words, especially to his grandmother.

'I think I'm falling in love with her.'

Nani took a small sip of her drink. A few seconds passed and the silence in the room became heavy, punctuated only by the sound of Angad's soft snoring. In the quiet of the room, Arjun processed the words he had just spoken. He had never said that about anyone, not even thought it. But now that the words were out, he was certain that he had never meant anything more.

When Nani finally spoke, her words brimmed with confidence. 'A Patiala man always gets his girl.'

With that, she clinked her glass with her grandson's and guzzled down the rest of her drink.

PART THREE
THE SCANDAL

Scandal Day 1

8.48 a.m.

Risha woke up in a good mood.

She had stayed up late sorting through nearly half the images from the shoot and was optimistic about sending the first set of thumbnails to Nitisha and Rohan by the end of the week. Risha had a head start on her photography work, no backlog on her *NT* work *and* she had a date with Arjun tonight.

It was only after stepping out of the auto that Risha realized she hadn't haggled with the auto wala. Not even getting ripped off by twenty bucks could dampen her spirits today.

So it was only natural that she dismissed Nidhi's 'SOS' text as hyperbole. Nidhi was probably just freaking out over Starbucks no longer serving their festive specials. Sure, they were delicious, but how many toffee nut lattes could a person drink?

It was only when the second text came that Risha began to wonder if Nidhi's anxiety was driven by something other than caffeine withdrawal.

Do NOT panic. I'll finish my morning meeting and see you in fifteen minutes. We'll figure this out.

Risha replied:

> Figure what out?

Nidhi wrote back:

> You haven't seen the paper???

What in the world had Nidhi so riled up? Had Salman Khan had another run-in with the law? Risha responded:

> Nope, was running late this morning. Let me grab a copy.

Nidhi's reply was instant:

> I'll meet you at the chai wala in ten. Hang in there, Rish.

Risha reached for the newspaper and sank into her chair, going through the front page. Something about the prime minister's latest international trip to Nicaragua.

She skimmed her way to the sports page, wondering if there was some news about Vikram. Nothing there either.

She flipped opened *Delhi Today*. The front page had pictures of Kareena and Saif holding hands, walking down Rodeo Drive in LA. Which meant that if Risha had been in LA *this* week instead of the previous one, she might've spotted them! But that seemed more worthy of a 'WTF' text than an 'SOS' text.

Which could only mean one thing. Page 3.

Risha flipped the page and stared at it in horror.

The top of Page 3 shouted '*Delhi Today* Exclusive!' in bold red letters followed by a full-page photo essay of the Khanna–Singhal wedding.

Private photos of the bride, groom and their respective families adorned the page. An intimate image of Nitisha and Rohan kissing captioned 'NitRo explosion'. A photo of Vikram and Rohan doing jaeger bombs together titled 'What a shot!'. An image of Vikram with Pinku titled 'Vikram Walia with Patiala-based entrepreneur Pankaj Sabharwal'. A photo of Vikram playing pinball captioned 'Bowled over!'. One too many photos of Vikram. A close-up of Arjun and Divya smiling at each other titled 'Arjun Khanna's latest conquest'. A shot of a teary-eyed Arvind Khanna hugging his daughter. A mini collage of Priye Ma and her clan. Clear, high-resolution photos. Dozens and dozens of photos. Photos undoubtedly taken by Risha.

She looked through the page and found a near-invisible footnote: 'The above images have been printed with permission from the Khanna family.'

And next to the picture of Arjun and Divya, written sideways in microscopic but legible font, were the words 'Photo credit: Candy'.

Suddenly the air in Risha's cubicle felt thick and muggy. She stepped out into the corridor, clutching the newspaper in her hands, and ran straight into Kabir.

'Hello, stranger,' he smiled. 'Hope you're impressed by my coup d'état!'

Risha looked at him, struggling to compose herself.

'Frankly,' Kabir continued, 'I was getting sick of Sukhi's pomposity and audacity. We'll just see how Sports beats *DT* after today's Page 3!'

'How did you get all these images?' Risha asked in a feeble voice.

'A good reporter never discloses his sources.' Kabir winked.

'Do you know who Candy is?' Risha croaked.

'Don't know, don't care.' Kabir shrugged.

'Then how did you get the images?' she asked again, her tone pleading.

'Hey, hey. Are you okay? You look distressed. Have you eaten breakfast? Do you want to step out for chai?' Kabir asked, placing a hand on her arm.

Risha winced at his touch, not wanting to be in his presence another moment. She took a deep breath and pulled herself together. 'No, I'm fine. I need to run down for something. I'll see you later.'

'Yes, let's do our weekly one-on-one around eleven?'

She nodded and scampered out of the building, desperate for some air. She sat on the cracked plastic stool outside the chai stall and stared at the newspaper in her hand. A moment later, she spotted Nidhi and jumped up. 'I didn't do this!'

Nidhi nodded. 'I know.'

'I promise it wasn't me, Nidhi!' Risha cried, her hands shaking.

'I believe you, Rish,' Nidhi said gently.

'I don't know how Kabir—how I—I mean where he—'

'Calm down,' Nidhi said, helping her sit back down on the stool.

'You don't understand. He won't be okay with this,' Risha said, taking the bottle of water Nidhi was handing her.

'Who cares what Kabir thinks?' Nidhi asked.

'Not Kabir! *Arjun*. He's a very private person and he won't be okay with his personal life being showcased like common gossip. This whole thing makes me look like an unprofessional, gold-digging, fame-hungry—'

'Stop talking,' Nidhi said firmly.

'I have no credibility left as a photographer. No one will ever trust me again. It's over, Nidhi,' Risha said, looking defeated.

'Don't be ridiculous,' Nidhi said with more conviction than she felt. 'It's a stupid misunderstanding and Arjun will understand that. As for your professional integrity, anyone with—'

'I was supposed to meet him today, but he'll think I did this. But I didn't, Nidhi. I swear!' Risha said emphatically.

'Risha, I'm going to say this for the last time, so listen carefully. I know you didn't do it. I don't know who did, but I'm going to find out. And as far as Arjun is concerned, call him and tell him the truth. I'm sure he's a reasonable guy and he'll hear you out. It will be okay,' Nidhi promised.

Risha nodded, sipping her water. After a few moments, when she had visibly calmed down, Nidhi spoke. 'At any point during the wedding, did you give your camera to anyone?'

Risha shook her head to say 'no'.

'Did you leave your camera lying around?'

'I would never leave my equipment . . .' Risha trailed off, remembering. 'After the cocktail party, I . . . I spent the night in Arjun's room.'

Nidhi raised a brow but didn't say anything.

'We fell asleep talking, nothing else,' Risha said. 'But I did leave my camera in my room. And in the morning, I found my memory card sitting on the table, which I found odd even at the time, because I couldn't remember taking it out.'

Nidhi took the newspaper from Risha and looked through the images again. 'There are no photos of the wedding day. So clearly someone "borrowed" your memory card the previous night and returned it before you could discover it was gone.'

Risha nodded in agreement. 'But who? And how did they get into my room?'

'They could've got a duplicate key card. I'm pretty sure people keep misplacing their keys during weddings,' Nidhi said, chewing on her lip thoughtfully. 'Will Kabir disclose his source?'

'No.'

'Any suspects?'

'It could be someone from SoL,' Risha guessed.

'Do you have photos of all the SoL members who attended the wedding?'

'I took a group photo at the mehndi—that has most of them.'

'Great, so that's a start. We can look through the Page 3 archives and find all their names,' Nidhi said, her jade eyes flashing with purpose.

Risha gave a little smile. 'And what will we do once we have their names, Sherlock?'

'We will "accidentally" stumble upon Kabir's email to corroborate the source,' Nidhi said.

Risha frowned. 'Firstly, are you sure you're not an investigative journalist? Secondly, what you're suggesting is illegal. And thirdly, even if it wasn't, how would we "accidentally stumble upon" his email?'

Nidhi shot her a confident smile. 'Oh, I think there's one particular IT guy who would be happy to do you a favour.'

Risha shook her head. 'I'm okay with looking through the archives, but I have to put my foot down at snooping through my boss's email.'

Realizing it was futile to try and convince Risha to do anything even remotely unscrupulous, Nidhi said, 'Let's table it for now.'

Risha stood up, feeling much better.

'You okay?' Nidhi asked.

'Yes,' Risha said. 'Or I will be after I make a phone call.'

'Arjun?'

Risha gave a nervous nod.

'I'm sure it will be fine. I'll see you at lunch?'

'Okay.'

She watched Nidhi disappear into their office building, then took a deep breath and dialled Arjun's number.

Arjun stood in his office, looking out the window. He had asked Annie Aunty to hold his calls for half an hour, but that was twenty minutes ago. Since then he'd been standing with his back to his large mahogany desk, staring at the skyline of the city his father had helped build. His cell phone buzzed and he glanced at it.

Risha Kohli.

For a moment he was tempted to pick up the phone and ram it against the wall with all his might. But he ignored it and continued to watch the traffic crawl on the highway. His phone rang again and he put it on silent mode before shoving it inside a drawer. Even reading her name felt like a dagger through his heart.

This morning, Arjun had woken up light-headed—one part hangover, one part Risha. The thought of meeting her tonight, making her laugh and holding her in his arms had him wide awake at 5 a.m. The mild headache had disappeared after his morning run, but the warm feeling inside him had only augmented. He'd nearly sent her a text, but then decided against it, not wanting to wake her up. Now he was glad he hadn't texted her, because he would've seemed like such a fool—back-stabbed, yet besotted.

As per his morning routine, Arjun had read the mainline and financial newspapers during breakfast. And if it wasn't for his mother's text, he would've skipped the entertainment supplements, as usual. However, Amrita's message at 7.30 a.m. had confused him, not only because she seldom woke up that early, but also because her message said 'Love your pics in *Delhi Today*!' It took Arjun a minute to figure out what *Delhi Today* was and another minute to find it under the pile of other newspapers. When he finally came across the pictures in question, he felt like someone had punched him in the stomach.

His first reaction was shock—complete disbelief that Risha had done this to him. She couldn't have, this was some kind of mistake. Except it wasn't. The only person who had access to all those photographs was Risha.

Had the last few days just been a game for her? Had she felt nothing for him in the time they had spent together? Had he really been so wrong about her?

His shock gave way to a feeling of betrayal. He remembered the envelope the security guard had handed her the night Arjun had dropped her home. She had clasped it to her chest like it contained state secrets, but now he realized it probably contained photographs from the wedding. Had she been planning on printing those photos in the newspaper, even as she kissed him a few minutes later?

And that's when the feeling of betrayal turned into anger. Blind white fury. By splashing those pictures in the newspaper, Risha had made him look like a fool, but she had also turned Chinky's wedding into a cheap PR stunt. To the world, it would look like Khanna Developers and Shopcart had tapped into their marketing budgets to release a full-page ad in the newspaper.

In his rage, Arjun had picked up his coffee mug and hurled it on the floor. The cook had come running out of the kitchen, looking frightened out of his wits. Arjun had mumbled an apology and helped him clear the mess. But unfortunately, the violence didn't help calm his temper. Because his anger wasn't directed at Risha for her connivance or cruelty; rather, it was directed at himself for his naiveté and stupidity. And for being duped by a woman, *again*.

Arjun's thoughts drifted to his ex-girlfriend Karishma. The previous year, he had pulled some strings to help her snag a shampoo brand endorsement with actor Nasser Khan. In addition to a month-long television campaign, Karishma's face (and overly Photoshopped hair) had been plastered on every newspaper, magazine and hoarding in town.

Soon after, she received an offer to do a cameo in a TV serial. Wanting to congratulate her on her success,

Arjun had flown to Mumbai to surprise her. But as fate would have it, he was the one in for a surprise. Arjun had walked into her hotel room to find her fucking Khan on the couch.

'I'm sorry, baby. I don't think we should see each other any more,' she said, and then went right back to what she was doing. The next day, *Bombay Times* had printed a picture of Karishma and Nasser having dinner at Hakkasan.

Arjun was probably the only asshole in the world who had his heart broken via a newspaper *twice*, he thought with self-deprecating humour. The only difference between the two women was that the model had sold her body and the journalist had sold her soul.

He turned at the soft knock on his door, knowing only one person would dare to disturb his solitude.

'Come in, Annie Aunty.'

'Your sister is on the phone,' she said laconically.

'I'll call her back later.'

'Do you still want me to hold your calls?' she asked.

Arjun shook his head. 'Give me five minutes and then send in Saraf,' he said, referring to the CFO.

She paused. 'Do you need anything else?'

He gestured to the coffee table on the other side of the room. 'Get rid of all the newspapers.'

Risha sent another message to Arjun, her seventh since morning. In addition to several texts, she had called him half a dozen times, but hadn't heard back from him. It was now 7 p.m. and she was, quite frankly, tired of his attitude. She had half a mind to march down to his apartment and confront him. At least he could've had the decency to call and cancel their date. How could he blacklist her without even hearing her version? How old was he anyway, ignoring her like that?

Then she felt a stab of guilt. The indisputable fact of the matter was that it was Risha's fault. She had left her camera unattended and, if the photos had made it to the newspaper, she was the one to blame. And she was willing to take responsibility for her actions, if only he would let her.

Risha swallowed her pride and typed him an email, having procured his email address from the business editor, Vandana, at the pretext of doing a follow-up on the photo essay.

'I don't think you'll get much out of him,' Vandana said. 'He's a bit . . . reticent.'

'I know,' Risha said with some annoyance.

'You do?'

'I mean, I've heard,' she amended with a smile before making a hasty exit from Vandana's room.

She sent Arjun the following email:

Can we please meet today? Just for a few minutes, so we can talk about this like adults. I know you're upset, but at least give me an opportunity to explain. Please call me!

A few minutes later, Risha received the following email from one Annabelle Dias:

Dear Ms Kohli,

I am writing to you on behalf of Mr Khanna.

Your constant communication in the form of phone
calls, text messages and emails is badgering, distasteful
and bordering on harassment. I request you to cease
contact with Mr Khanna immediately or he will be
forced to undertake legal action against you.
We hope to resolve this issue promptly and amicably.

Sincerely,
Annabelle Dias
Assistant to the CEO, Khanna Developers

Risha had been on the edge the entire day and that email
was enough to send her over. She wrote a text to Nidhi:

Mission SoL Spy is off. Please don't ask me why. I
don't want to talk about Arjun Khanna ever again.
I'm sorry I ever met him.

Nidhi texted back:

What happened?

Risha forwarded the email to Nidhi with a line of her own:

I mean it, Nidhi. I never want to speak about him. EVER.

Furious on her friend's behalf, Nidhi responded:

I second that. However, it would be nice to drop an
email to Nitisha and Rohan.

Risha agreed with that. She had spent the whole day fretting
over Arjun's reaction, not realizing that the newly married

couple was the most affected party in all this. She wrote them a short note explaining about the memory card and apologizing profusely. She assumed complete responsibility for the day's events, ending the email with the following line:

> I know you have no reason to believe me, but please do.
> I promise you I had nothing to do with it. I'm truly sorry.

Nitisha and Rohan were due to leave for their honeymoon in two weeks, but since it was the day after their wedding, Risha knew she probably wouldn't hear from them for a while. So she was surprised when Rohan's reply came mere minutes later:

> Risha, we know you didn't. Lack of privacy is one of the perils of being in the public eye and we must endure it as best as we can.
> Nitisha says she can't wait to see the first set of pictures!

Risha exhaled in relief. It was the first easy breath she had taken since the morning.

Scandal Day 5

4.13 a.m.

Arjun awoke with a start.

He glanced at the digital clock on his nightstand. As usual, he had beaten his alarm. He wondered how he had ever managed to oversleep the morning of the wedding. And then he remembered.

Risha.

He remembered the way she felt wrapped in his arms. He remembered nestling his chin in the nook of her neck.

He remembered the way she smelled, like frangipanis on a rainy afternoon. He remembered her bright hazel eyes glittering with laughter at something he had said. And then he remembered the garish photo collage in the newspaper.

Arjun threw back his comforter and sat up in bed. Trying to ignore the throbbing in his head, he grabbed his phone to look through his emails. The interior designer had sent him the proposed design of the model apartment for the new building. As he waited for the image to download, he skimmed through his inbox, but found nothing of consequence. Then again, he had only checked his email three hours earlier.

While searching for the downloaded photo in his phone, Arjun spotted the selfie of Risha and himself, and his hold on his phone tightened.

How could anyone who looked so innocent be so calculating? He stared at her beguiling eyes and seemingly sincere smile, and thought, with a whit of remorse, that perhaps he had jumped the gun with the threat of legal action. Her texts had sounded so ingenuous that he had nearly called her back. Which is the reason he had asked Annie Aunty to draft an official-sounding mail. He had almost hoped that Risha would call his bluff, but the phone calls and texts had stopped immediately.

He tossed his phone on the bed and got ready for his run. Instead of the usual runners' track in his building, Arjun stepped out on to Golf Course Road. Maybe the few extra kilometres would help subside the pounding in his head.

And the ache in his chest.

'Hello?' Risha answered her desk phone.

'Madam, there is someone here to meet you,' said the security guard from the reception.

Risha frowned. 'I don't have any appointments. Who is it?'

'I don't know, madam. He has a delivery and he said he will only give it to you.'

Risha's heart skipped a beat. Maybe it was Arjun. Maybe he had realized her innocence and had come to apologize for jumping to conclusions.

Risha stood up hurriedly and slammed the phone, drawing a sharp look from Kabir. She threw him an apologetic smile and walked to the reception—hopped, was more like it. She opened the door and saw her nineteen-year-old cousin, Bobby.

'Hi, Bobby,' she said, surprised. What was he doing here? Were Chachi and Chacha okay?

'Hi, Didi!' he said with a bright smile.

'What are you doing here?' she asked and then, trying to conceal her disappointment that he wasn't Arjun, added cheerily, 'It's so good to see you!'

'Likewise, Didi. Actually, your dad sent me this courier and asked me to hand-deliver it, since you didn't receive his last few packages,' Bobby explained.

Risha remembered saying that to her father the last time he had asked her opinion on so-and-so boy as a potential husband.

'You came all the way from North Campus to Connaught Place for *this*?' Risha asked, feeling terribly guilty for the inconvenience her little white lie had caused him. Her parents were going to get an earful for this.

Bobby shook his head. 'No, no, I take MBA coaching classes across the street, so I thought I would drop it off before class.'

'Oh, thanks, Bobby. And sorry for the trouble.'

'No formalities, Didi. *Ghar ki baat hai*,' Bobby assured her.

Even though Risha knew it was a casually uttered platitude, his choice of words suddenly made her very homesick. Wanting to extend her meeting with her cousin, she asked, 'Do you want to come in for some chai?'

'I can't, I'm late for class. But next time, pukka!' Bobby promised with a grin.

Risha gave him a quick hug and thanked him again before waving goodbye.

With a sigh, she opened the envelope, dreading its contents.

Delhi University Boys' Hostel courier log
Sender's name: Dr A.K. Kohli, Amritsar
Receiver's name: Maneesh Kohli, New Delhi
Date of receipt: Mar 2, 2016
Time stamp: 3:51 PM

> Extremely handsome and energetic Punjabi doctor (27, 5'8") having own nursing home in Patiala seeks Hindu/Sikh girl, doctor preferred but non-doctors welcome to apply. Girl should be homely and cultured. No dowry. Contact: dr_romeo311@hotmail.co.in

There was another listing below that, but Risha's eyes had started burning at the word 'Patiala', so she stopped reading. For a split second, she was tempted to email Dr Romeo. Maybe this was her fate, becoming a homely and cultured wife to an energetic doctor. Maybe she should move back to Amritsar, and with it, to a simpler life.

The hardest decision she ever had to make back in Amritsar was whether to stuff herself with popcorn at Rialto Cinema or gorge on kachoris at Giani Tea Stall. She thought of the time Rishabh had taught her to drive a scooter. She had fallen smack in the middle of the crowded Lawrence Road, badly scraped her knee and stubbornly refused to cry when her father dressed her wound.

Suddenly, Risha missed her parents terribly. Her independence felt like loneliness and the space of the proverbial big city made her claustrophobic. She crushed the newspaper clipping in her hand, then feeling guilty because Bobby had made the effort to hand deliver it, straightened it between the palms of her hands and shoved it inside her purse.

For the rest of the day, Risha threw herself in her work. 11 Foods with the Most Antioxidants. 6 Reasons Power Yoga Trumps Gym. 8 Ways to Fall Asleep Faster.

When she sent Kabir her third piece, he came by her desk. 'Whoa there, slow down, tiger!'

She looked at him inquiringly.

'I have a strong feeling you're planning a holiday,' he said.

'Why?'

'Because you're obviously trying to get a head start on work,' he said, referring to her back-to-back articles.

'You didn't like them?' Risha asked.

'Au contraire. It's some of your best work. But if you have so much time on your hands, why don't you help with Page 3?' Kabir suggested.

Risha smiled sweetly. 'Thanks, but no thanks.'

'Okay, but stop writing faster than I can read,' he teased.

An hour later, Nidhi met Risha at the exit gate of the *News Today* building and tried to convince her to come over for dinner. 'We'll make it quick, I promise,' Nidhi said, as they walked towards the parking lot.

Risha shook her head again. 'I have a ton of work.'

Nidhi cocked her head. 'I thought you wrote three pieces today?'

'Photography work,' Risha clarified.

'The Khanna–Singhal wedding?'

'Yup.'

'Why's that so urgent?' Nidhi asked, as they reached her car.

'I want to get the first set of photos across to Nitisha and Rohan before they leave for their honeymoon,' Risha explained.

Nidhi frowned. 'But they don't leave until next week. Can't you do it tomorrow?'

'I could, but frankly, I'm quite tired of looking at Arjun Khanna's face,' Risha said, forcing a laugh.

Nidhi caught the pained look in Risha's eyes before her friend ducked in through the passenger door. 'So have you received any more entertaining matrimonial ads from your parents?'

Risha dug into her purse for the newspaper clipping. 'This will crack you up, for sure!'

Nidhi managed to keep a straight face as Risha read out the matrimonial. Or at least until she got to the email ID.

'*Dr Romeo*?' Nidhi gasped, through a fit of giggles.

'Careful. That's my future husband you're talking about,' Risha said with a wry smile.

'Maybe it's an old email address, from when he was a kid,' Nidhi reasoned.

'Must be, because who the hell still uses Hotmail?' Nidhi glanced at the cut-out in Risha's hand. 'What about the second one?'

'A tissue paper magnate,' Risha answered, skimming through the listing.

'What's wrong with him?' Nidhi asked.

'Nothing.'

Except that he didn't make her laugh. Or bring her desserts. Or make the world stop spinning on its axis every time he touched her.

'Maybe you should meet this tissue paper guy,' Nidhi suggested.

'Yes, because if I married him, we could use our unlimited supply of paper products to toilet-paper Sukhi's cabin. What say?' Risha grinned.

Nidhi casually flicked the clipping from Risha's hand and tossed it into the car's cup holder. 'And we could blame it on Kabir!'

That made Risha laugh.

Four hours and three hundred photos later, Risha began to see the merits of meeting a new guy. She touched her hand to her laptop screen and could almost feel Arjun's scruffy jaw under her fingertips. Maybe this wouldn't be so hard if he wasn't so outrageously handsome, she thought with grim humour.

She was such an idiot! How could she be with a guy who had cast her aside over a stupid misunderstanding, without so much as giving her an opportunity to explain? Not that he *wanted* to be with her.

A tear rolled down Risha's cheek. Maybe having the tissue paper guy around wasn't such a bad idea.

Scandal Day 9

7.23 p.m.

Arjun walked into his apartment and found his sister and brother-in-law lounging on his couch, a stack of papers in their hands.

'Hey, guys,' he said, smiling his first genuine smile in a week.

Observing his four-day-old stubble and dishevelled hair, Nitisha said, 'You look like crap.'

'Nice to see you too, Chinky,' Arjun said dryly.

'Just saying.' She shrugged.

Rohan got up to shake his hand. 'Dude, I get the whole unshaven look, but what's with the hair?'

'I fell asleep in the car,' Arjun explained.

'Not while driving, I hope,' Rohan joked.

Arjun shook his head. 'Driver.'

'I thought you hate being "driven around like a child",' Nitisha said, biting into an apple.

'I haven't been sleeping much at night, so I asked to borrow Dad's driver,' Arjun said.

Nitisha and Rohan exchanged a look.

'The office is ten minutes from here. Are you telling me you've only been getting two ten-minute naps a day?' Nitisha asked, her face filled with worry.

'Did you guys break into my apartment to lecture me on sleep?' Arjun snapped.

'Nitisha wanted to show you the wedding photos,' Rohan said. 'And we didn't break in, we used the all-access key card.'

Arjun tossed his laptop bag on a chair, flopped on to the chaise of his sectional sofa and stretched his legs. Nitisha handed him a large sheet of photo paper, containing a dozen thumbnails arranged neatly next to each other. The three of them pored over the photos for a few minutes, making jokes about the SoL clan's poses and Pinku's dense chest hair, until Nitisha pointed to one particular photo. 'This one is my favourite.'

The photo was of Nitisha seated on the couch in the bridal suite on the morning of her choora. There was a large mirror on the wall behind her and it reflected the happy expressions of her entire family.

'Yes, it's a good one,' Arjun agreed.

'*Really* good,' Nitisha said, meaningfully. 'Have you seen it properly?'

Arjun narrowed his eyes and studied the photo carefully. He was about to ask her what she was talking about when he spotted something. On the right corner of the mirror, crouched on the floor, her face half hidden by her camera, was Risha.

Arjun dropped the photograph like it was on fire and stood up abruptly. 'I think I've seen enough.'

'Bhai, have you spoken to Risha?' Nitisha asked softly.

'I'm not interested in speaking to lying, conniving con artists,' he bit out.

Nitisha shook her head. 'She's not a liar. Risha had nothing—'

'I don't want to talk about this,' Arjun said tersely.

'But you don't understand. Her memory card—'

'That's enough, Nitisha!' Arjun roared.

Nitisha pressed back into the sofa, aghast. She had never seen her brother so angry.

A few moments later, Rohan stood up and put a hand on Arjun's shoulder. 'I think you owe your sister an apology,' he said in a quiet voice.

Arjun took a deep breath. 'I'm sorry, Chinky. I shouldn't have raised my voice.'

Nitisha shook her head. 'It's okay, Bhai. I just hate seeing you like . . . *this*.'

'I promise I'll shave,' he teased.

She gave him a small smile, but it didn't reach her eyes. 'I'm going down to say hi to Mom and Dad. Rohan, do you want to come?'

Rohan nodded. 'Go on. I'll be there in a few minutes.'

After she left, Rohan turned to Arjun with a speculative look. 'Drink?'

Arjun shook his head. Then he nodded.

Ignoring his ambivalent response, Rohan poured two large whiskies and brought them over to the coffee table. They sipped their drinks in comfortable silence for several minutes, until Rohan finally spoke. 'What's going on, man?'

Arjun stared at the bottom of his glass. 'Work stuff.'

The deep lines of fatigue on Arjun's face and the lost look in his eyes made it obvious to Rohan that there was more on his brother-in-law's mind than just 'work stuff'. So Rohan decided not to beat around the bush. 'She didn't do it.'

Arjun didn't pretend not to understand. 'Then who did?'

'I don't know, but I'm positive it wasn't Risha.'

The conviction in Rohan's voice took Arjun by surprise. 'What makes you so sure?'

'Because she told me.'

'And that's enough?'

'When you choose to trust somebody, you can't have conditions. You need to trust them completely, no questions asked.'

Arjun gave a mirthless laugh. 'Are you sure it's not just because she's a friend of Vikram's?'

'Are you sure you want to let her go over a small misunderstanding?' Rohan asked.

Arjun's jaw hardened. 'Even if she didn't do it, it doesn't matter. She's just a wedding photographer.'

'That's true. *Just* a wedding photographer. Not someone worth losing sleep over.'

Arjun shot him a look.

'Look, man,' Rohan began, 'if you want an out, you have it. But if you genuinely like this girl, you need to let her in.'

'I *don't* love her!' Arjun said fiercely.

Rohan smiled. He hadn't used the word 'love'. 'Of course, you don't.'

Arjun chugged the rest of his drink and Rohan took that as his cue to leave.

'Time for a meet-and-greet with the in-laws,' Rohan said, standing up.

Arjun gave him a grim smile and walked him to the elevator. 'Take care, man.'

'You, too. Sleep well.'

If only, Arjun thought. If only.

Scandal Day 10

9.09 a.m.

Arjun washed down the last of his breakfast with his coffee and stood up. He folded the newspaper into a quarter and tossed it on the dining table, before slipping into his jacket. As he walked over to the living room to pick up his laptop, the collage of photos on the coffee table caught his eye. Having missed the cricket match, he picked up the sheet containing photos of the event. One image in particular caught his attention—a picture of Team Bride in a huddle.

The team members included his father, two of his golf buddies (a high court judge and the CEO of the largest bank in the country), Pinku and Minku, Annie Aunty's husband, Khanna Heights's property manager, Shankar the driver, and even Asif, the gardener's son. They seemed to be in the midst of an intense team strategy discussion and were oblivious to being photographed.

In fact, Arjun wondered how Risha had taken the shot without being noticed. She had probably crouched on the field, snuck her hand through one of the gaps between the players' legs and pointed the camera upwards to take the picture. He felt a reluctant flicker of respect for Risha. Irrespective of what had transpired between them, he couldn't help but admire her commitment to her craft.

'The party was still on and I didn't want to miss another Tetris face-off,' she had told him at four in the morning.

'I don't know how long Priye Ma will be, is it okay if Rishabh comes up and waits here for a bit?' she had requested Nitisha on the night of the mehndi.

'*I can't drink, I'm working,*' she had said on several occasions.

Arjun remembered Rohan's first impression of her. '*She was so forthcoming about being a novice. She could have concealed her inexperience; instead she volunteered the truth.*'

A strange feeling gnawed at Arjun. All those did not sound like the words of a liar. His thoughts were interrupted by a call from his CFO, Naina Saraf. 'What's up, Saraf?'

'Have you seen the fucking *Economic Times*?' she asked.

'Yes,' he answered, ignoring the profanity. Saraf didn't mean disrespect; that was just how she talked. The newspaper had done a piece on how the delay in sand supplies would affect various real estate projects in NCR.

'It's only a matter of time before they pick up on the bloody strike. This is not looking good for our bottom line, Arjun,' she said. 'We have another meeting scheduled with Yadav and his team today; we need to fix this shit show.'

'I think,' Arjun said, formulating his thoughts as he spoke, 'I have an idea to fix it.'

'Better be the best goddamn idea you've ever had,' Saraf said.

Arjun relayed his plan to her and she was shocked. 'You're not fucking serious?'

'As a heart attack. I'll be at the office in fifteen minutes, let's talk about it then,' he said, hanging up the phone.

Then he sent a text to Rohan:

I need Vikram's number.

Scandal Day 11

2.01 a.m.

Risha answered her phone without looking at the screen. 'Yes, Rishabh? How may I be of service to you at this unearthly hour?'

'Hi, Kohli! Were you asleep?'

'Of course, not. Who in their right mind is asleep at two in the morning?' she said, feigning astonishment.

'Achha, I'm coming up. Open the door,' he whispered.

'What! Are you serious? How did you get past Tyagiji?' she asked, flying out of bed to unlock the door.

'I didn't have to. He's asleep!' her friend said, hugging her as he entered the apartment.

'Huh?' Risha said, intrigued by this new development.

'I did spot an empty quarter of Royal Challenge at his window, maybe that had something to do with it,' Rishabh guessed, making a mental note to bring the unrelenting guard a full bottle of the whisky next time.

'What are you doing here?' she asked.

'I need some advice,' he said, flopping on the leather bean bag, causing it to make a 'poof' sound.

'Advice that clearly could not wait till the *morning*.'

'*Were* you sleeping?' he challenged.

Actually, she'd been lying in bed for two hours staring at the ceiling.

'I was about to,' she evaded, sprawling next to him on the floor. 'Besides, since when do you take advice from me?'

'I've been offered a movie!'

'No way!' she said, her face lighting up with excitement.

'I was at Chateau when this *really* hot man—fifty-something, salt-and-pepper hair—comes up to me and asks if I want to be in a movie—'

'Who's the director? Who are the other actors? What's the story? When will—'

'Let me finish, woman! Naturally, I asked him all these questions and he said he'd love to share all the details over dinner tomorrow night at the Leela Hotel, which is incidentally where he's staying. So I—'

'So you want to know whether or not you should go?' she pre-empted.

'Of course I'm going, Kohli! I want to know what I should *wear*,' he finished.

'Please tell me you're joking,' she said.

'About what?' he asked.

'About going! Are you insane? Didn't you read the *NT* exposé about old men luring young models to their five-star hotel rooms with promises of advertising campaigns and big banner films? It's obviously a set-up!'

Rishabh shrugged. 'I know.'

His words chilled her to the bone.

'You can't be serious,' Risha rasped.

He looked up at her and the dejection in his eyes filled her with sympathy. She let the silence in the room linger before speaking in a calming voice. 'Rishabh, you're better than this. I know you've been struggling for a long time, but the hard work *will* pay off. I believe in you and you need to believe in yourself, too.'

He sighed. 'It's just so hard sometimes, Kohli. When the world keeps telling you that you're mediocre long enough, you start believing it.'

'You're not mediocre. You just did a campaign for Delhi's largest fashion retailer!' she argued.

'But I want to do a movie. And it's not like all the other models are so clean! Everyone is—'

'I don't care if every single model in the country is sleeping around to get roles. You don't have to do it.'

'I know, but a lot of people are doing it, and it seems to be working really well for them. So maybe . . .'

'Look,' Risha said gently, 'if you want me to say it's okay, I'm not going to. And I think that's the reason you came here at this hour—because you knew I would tell you it's not okay. You will succeed on your own merit and you don't have to stoop to doing stuff like this.'

He buried his face in his hands and groaned. 'I thought I was going to be a movie star.'

Rishabh was the closest thing Risha had to a sibling, and seeing his slumped shoulders and despondent look broke her heart. She put her arms around him. 'You will be, someday. Just not tomorrow.'

He nodded. 'I can't believe I almost got roofied.'

Risha choked. 'Rishabh!'

'No, seriously, Kohli. Imagine if you hadn't answered the phone or if you'd been asleep,' he said, looking horrified. 'What if I'd gone to meet that guy and—'

'But I *did* answer my phone, I *wasn't* asleep and you're *not* going to meet him,' she said, taking his hand to put a stop to his wild imaginings.

He nodded and squeezed her hand.

'Look at us.' Risha sighed after a few minutes of silence. 'A couple of losers, wide awake at two in the morning, prophesying about what might have been.'

Rishabh looked up suddenly. 'What do you mean?'

'Nothing,' she said, standing up. 'Do you want chai?'

He watched her carefully guarded expression. 'Sure.'

She grabbed a pot from a shelf in the kitchen and filled it with water.

'By the way,' Rishabh began casually, 'why *were* you awake so late? I hope you're not fretting over Arjun Khanna's "latest conquest"?'

Risha dropped the tin of tea leaves on the counter, causing a loud clatter.

Oh, so *that* was on her mind.

'Don't believe everything you read on Page 3, Kohli.'

'I don't,' Risha said. 'He's not seeing that girl. And even if he is, it doesn't make a difference to me.'

'Yes, she doesn't seem like the type of girl he— OHMYGOD! I totally forgot!' Rishabh exclaimed, leaping off the bean bag and practically sprinting to the kitchen. He whipped out his phone and started skimming through his Facebook photos. 'You'll never guess what I found the other day! I was looking at last year's Gladrags after-party pictures—remember that guy, whatshisname, had taken them? What *was* his name? Something like Sandeep or Sanjeev or something . . .'

Grateful for the change in subject and for the therapeutic sound of her friend's rambling, Risha brewed the tea with perfunctory accuracy. She tuned out his struggle to remember 'that guy's' name, and was nodding absently until Rishabh said, 'And that's when I figured out where I'd heard the name Arjun Khanna before!'

'Where?'

'Don't you listen to anything I say? The *photo*,' he said pointing to his phone. 'Sanjay had introduced us, but it was just like a quick hi-hello. I remember Arjun wasn't the talkative type and mostly kept to himself, but Karishma kept flaunting him the whole night. Arjun Khanna *this* and Arjun Khanna *that*,' he said, gesticulating dramatically. 'She must've said his name at least a million times!'

Risha took the phone from his hand and peered at the screen. The image was a little hazy and even though his gaze was averted from the camera, the man in the photo was definitely Arjun.

Ever since Risha had handed over the first set of wedding photos to Nitisha and Rohan, she had announced the chapter of Arjun Khanna officially closed. She had sworn not to torture herself by staring at his pictures for hours and she hadn't broken that resolve even once.

But now, looking at his face sent a flood of emotions raging through her.

As always, Arjun was dressed impeccably and his trademark five o'clock shadow only accentuated his handsome, chiselled features. His dark eyes were twinkling with humour and his hard jaw was softened just barely by a half-smile. Even in this pixelated profile shot, he exuded charm and confidence.

And then there was the girl clinging to his arm. With her Victoria Beckhamesque bob cut, flaming red lips and glamorous halter sequin dress, she was the very soul of poise and élan. In comparison, Risha felt gauche and small-town.

Risha returned the phone, and because looking at Arjun's picture wasn't masochistic enough, she asked, 'What was she like?'

Rishabh took a seat on the kitchen counter and sipped his tea. 'Total bitch,' he said, matter-of-factly.

She frowned. 'You say that about everyone.'

'I'm serious, Kohli. She was the most vile creature I've ever laid my eyes on. Arrogant, narcissistic and opportunistic as hell. Everyone hated her, the guys *and* the girls. We were all thrilled when Karishma left Delhi, because she was the type of girl that would slit her own mother's throat to get ahead in life. Slit her mother's throat or suck her fa—'

'Okay, okay, I get it!' Risha said, raising her palms. 'No need to get graphic.'

'Anyway, she did some big face cream or hair oil campaign with Nasser Khan and now she's going to be in a movie. Like, *Raaz 8* or something. Can you believe it? That silicon-implanted, butt-augmented, hair-extended little slut is going to be a movie star! And I'm going to be posing for Frontier Bazaar billboards for the rest of my life,' Rishabh groaned.

'Well, I think Frontier is a great brand to endorse. They always offer me masala nimbu pani when I shop at their store.'

'Nice to know that anyone can buy your loyalty for a glass of nimbu pani.'

Risha was offended by that. 'Hey! *Masala* nimbu pani.'

Scandal Day 13

7.51 p.m.

At the Gurgaon Golf Club, Arjun sank into a chair next to Vikram, a huge smile on his face. 'I had no idea cricket was so much fun.'

'You're pretty good. Did you play as a kid?' the cricketer asked.

'I'm more of a football guy,' Arjun confessed.

'Me too,' Vikram joked, and Arjun laughed.

On the day of the *Economic Times* article, Arjun had asked Yadav and his team to a friendly cricket match.

'Is this going to be like *Lagaan*, Bhaiyaji?' Yadav had wondered.

'On the contrary,' Arjun assured him, 'we're going to play together, not on opposing teams.'

Yadav was puzzled by that. 'So what are the stakes?'

'No stakes, no strings. Just a fun game of cricket. Half the players in each team will be Khanna Developers employees and half will be your guys.'

'But how will that work?' Yadav had asked, looking concerned.

'Don't worry, it will work,' Arjun promised.

The twenty-over game had finished two hours ago, with Vikram batting for one of the teams. Just *seeing* Vikram had the workers up in a frenzy, let alone the thought of playing a cricket match with him. The match had been a close one, with one team beating the other by only five runs. After the match, the workers and their families had swarmed Vikram, who had patiently obliged their requests for photographs. A few minutes later, Yadav took the stage to announce that the strike was off.

Arjun's first instinct had been to call Risha and tell her about his day, about his big win.

'Sometimes people just want to feel like . . . people. They want to believe that, in the larger scheme of things, they matter.'

Risha's simple advice, combined with her compelling photographs, had helped Arjun come up with the idea of the cricket match.

In the days since the newspaper article, Arjun had spent every waking hour and every sleepless night agonizing over it, and he was absolutely certain that Risha had nothing to do with the appearance of Chinky's wedding photos in the newspaper.

He'd been too angry to see it earlier, but if she had really sold him out, the photo credit would carry her own name, not the silly alias Nani had given her. But frankly, even if it *had* carried Risha's name, Arjun would not believe she was anything but innocent.

Arjun had played back snatches from their first conversation in his head over and over again.

'My cousin showed the couple some of my photos and they liked my work. Plus, it was cheaper to fly me from India than to hire a local photographer.' Arjun was the brother of a client and she could've easily omitted the latter half of that statement. But she hadn't.

'I haven't technically paid for this seat. I thought it would be unfair to take advantage of a fortuitous situation,' she'd told him because she would rather spend the entire flight being miserable than do something that she considered vaguely unscrupulous. Something that, for most people, would have been a no-brainer.

Risha was probably the only person her age who honoured a bunch of archaic rules set by her parents, even in their absence. *'There was no other way they would let their only child move to the big bad city all by herself. It's a small price to pay.'*

And finally, Arjun couldn't get her innocent confession out of his head. The poignant admission in his hotel room that had knocked the wind out of him. *'I'm . . . I'm a little nervous.'*

Risha was incapable of telling even a small, harmless lie, never mind concocting an elaborate scheme to hurt someone. If anyone was inviolable, Risha was. Arjun owed her a big apology and he intended to make it immediately.

But first, he owed the vice captain of the Indian cricket team a drink.

'I can't thank you enough for this, man,' Arjun said again, clinking his lager glass with Vikram's.

'Don't worry about it. I'm happy to get some practice before the Sri Lanka tour,' Vikram said modestly, as though playing gully cricket with twenty amateurs was the best practice he could ever get. Arjun could see why Rohan was friends with the guy.

Vikram's phone beeped and he picked it up, laughing at something on his screen. 'Nidhi was out with some friends earlier today, she just sent me a picture,' he explained, turning the phone towards Arjun.

Four people stood beneath a poster of the latest superhero movie, imitating the actors' macho poses. He recognized Rishabh and Nidhi, they stood next to a guy wearing an Avengers sweatshirt. And finally, Risha. The Avengers guy had his arm around her as she flexed her 'muscles'.

She looked unbearably cute in the picture. And happy.

A feeling of panic struck Arjun. 'How is she?'

'She's good. She quit her job.'

Arjun was surprised. 'Risha quit her job?'

Vikram smiled. 'I was talking about Nidhi.'

Arjun gave an embarrassed nod and stared into his glass. 'Of course.'

'Risha is fine too. In fact,' Vikram added casually, 'I think she's meeting a guy today.'

Arjun's head jerked up. 'What guy?'

'Some guy her parents set her up with. Wait, let me show you the picture,' Vikram said, handing his phone to Arjun.

Arjun snatched the phone from Vikram, but instead of a Shaadi.com profile, he found himself looking at an image of a newspaper clipping.

> Delhi-based business family seeks match for their MBA son (28, 6') who handles the family's tissue paper products business. The girl should be well educated good-natured, family-oriented and have a sense of humour.
>
> Contact:
> admin@softex.com

Arjun's jaw dropped. 'Shit.'

'What?'

'I know this guy. I mean, I've met him once. His name is Dhruv and he's a friend of Angad's—they were in a family business programme together—and we met over drinks once, a long time ago.'

'Oh, that's great. Is he a nice guy?' Vikram asked, seeming genuinely interested.

'Yes, he is.' Arjun scowled.

Dhruv was a *great* guy. He was rich as Croesus, good-looking enough to be an underwear model, and if memory served right, funny too. He would make Risha very happy.

Arjun clenched his fists.

The *hell* he would. Not if Arjun had anything to do with it.

'Do you know when they are meeting?'

'For dinner, I guess.' Vikram shrugged, hiding a smile.

Arjun glanced at his watch; it was 8.30 p.m. They were probably having dinner as they spoke. Dhruv would probably be in love with Risha halfway through dessert.

And she could fall for him too.

Arjun stood up suddenly. 'Vikram, I'm really—'

'Let me guess. You want to cut our evening short?' Vikram said, looking very amused.

Arjun shot him an apologetic smile. 'I owe you one.'

Vikram gave him a friendly slap on the back. 'Oh, I think you do.'

Arjun drove from Gurgaon to Vasant Kunj in record time. As he pulled into the parking lot of Risha's building, his phone rang. At that moment, all Arjun wanted to do was find Risha, so he was tempted to ignore the call. But answering it turned out to be a good decision, because his father was on the phone and he sounded positively elated.

'Great job today, beta! I'm so proud of you,' Arvind gushed. 'You handled this very well.'

'Thanks, Dad,' Arjun said. 'I wasn't sure it would work, but I'm relieved it did.'

'Yes, it was a very creative solution. How did you get the idea?'

From the girl I'm going to marry.

'Please tell me it's not that Divya girl,' his father said, and Arjun realized he had spoken out loud.

Crap.

'Uh, no. Why would you say that?'

'That ridiculous garbage your mother got printed in the newspaper. It looked like a paid piece of—'

'Wait, what?'

'A paid piece of rubbish. Like we were using Chinky's wedding as a PR strategy to—'

'*Mom* did that?' Arjun yelled into the phone.

'Of course. Who else is capable?'

'Why?!' Arjun exploded.

'For her beloved Priye Ma. Apparently, SoL subscribes to the "any publicity is good publicity" school of thought,' his father explained.

'How did she do it?' Arjun asked, trying to keep his anger in check.

'She convinced that poor simpleton Pinku Sabharwal that having his picture printed in the paper would give his salwar business the marketing thrust it needs. Pinku helped her procure the photographs.'

'How did he manage that?' Arjun wondered, more to himself than to his father.

'No idea. But don't let it bother you. I'm just relieved you aren't marrying into the Sinha family.'

'Over my dead body,' Arjun assured him.

'That's my boy!' Arvind laughed. 'So who is this girl you're engaged to?'

'We're not engaged.'

'I thought you said you're going to marry her?'

'Eventually. But first I have to convince her that I'm worthy of her.'

The senior Khanna chuckled. 'I like her already.'

Two hours later, Arjun was pacing up and down outside Risha's apartment like a caged animal. For the millionth time, he ran the scenario through his head.

Risha and Dhruv having a great time at dinner, holding hands over their chocolate-based dessert, kissing passionately in the car. And Arjun didn't even want to think about what else they could be doing.

This was a really long date, he thought with frustration. She had no business being out with a guy for so long on a first date. Unless she really liked him.

Shit. What if she really liked him?

Arjun sat on the stairs opposite her door and shoved his hands in his hair.

He was an idiot. A complete and utter idiot for losing the only girl he had ever loved over something as meaningless as a bunch of Page 3 photographs. Arjun was willing to take every single photograph of him ever clicked and print it in the newspaper if it meant he could have Risha back.

If she showed up with Dhruv in tow, Arjun would have no choice but to kick the asshole's teeth in. Too bad if he was a 'nice guy'. But Arjun was being needlessly paranoid; there was no point imagining the worst.

Another fifteen minutes passed and Arjun was imagining the worst. That Risha was not coming home at all. That she was going home with Dhruv.

The elevator dinged and Risha walked out. *Alone*.

Arjun's heart slammed into his ribs. She was wearing the same clothes from the photo Vikram had shown him earlier today, and she looked beautiful. But sleep deprived.

Arjun felt a twinge of guilt.

Risha saw him and stopped dead in her tracks. Something like hope flickered in her eyes, but it was quickly replaced with indignation.

'What do you want?' she asked icily, putting her backpack down in front of her door.

'I want to talk,' Arjun said, hoping she wasn't too pissed off about Annie Aunty's email.

'You should've sent a subpoena.'

Okay, so she was pissed off about Annie Aunty's email.

'I'm sorry about that email,' he said.

'I'm a journalist.' She shrugged. 'If I don't receive at least one legal threat a week, my boss thinks I'm not working hard enough.'

Arjun fought back an admiring smile.

She began entering her apartment and he blurted, 'The strike was called off.'

A genuine look of relief crossed her face and she paused in the doorway. 'That's great! Congratulations.'

'I took your advice,' he said, trying to keep her from going inside.

That caught her attention. 'What do you mean?'

'I organized a cricket match with the contractor's men. And since Vikram was the surprise guest, the workers lapped it up!'

Her face broke into a genial smile. 'Nice! Oh, so that's why he didn't show up for the movie today.'

Which reminded him. 'How was your date?'

'My *what*?'

'Vikram said your parents introduced you to some guy,' Arjun said, hoping he didn't look as miserable as he felt.

'I don't think that's any of your business,' she said, ready to slam the door in his face.

'Risha, wait!' he said, blocking the door with his foot. 'I'm sorry. I . . . you're right. It's none of my business.'

Risha sighed. 'What are you *really* doing here?'

'I know you had nothing to do with the photographs in the newspaper.'

'What tipped you off? Surely not the dozen texts I sent you?' she said caustically, but Arjun saw traces of hurt in her eyes.

'*When you choose to trust somebody, you need to trust them completely.*'

It was time to let her in. 'Last year, I was dating a girl and, long story short, I found out that she'd been using me to advance her career. I caught her cheating on me, and since then I've had some . . . trust issues.'

Her face filled with compassion. 'I'm sorry.'

He shook his head. 'I was a fool.'

'I think,' she said staunchly, 'that *she* was the fool.'

And that's when Arjun realized why he loved Risha.

He had ignored her, threatened her, pretty much ostracized her, and yet her eyes were alight with allegiance. She immediately trusted his version, without asking for any additional information. Risha was innately kind, unquestioningly loyal and all-round perfect.

And Arjun did not deserve her.

'I shouldn't have shut you out,' he said, his handsome face ridden with remorse.

She nodded. 'Yes, you shouldn't have.'

'I'm sorry.'

'It's okay, I understand,' she said.

Arjun gazed into her eyes and, in a voice hoarse with emotion, said, 'I'm in love with you.'

Risha looked at him blankly.

When she said nothing, Arjun spoke in a defeated voice. 'I just want you to be happy. With Dhruv or . . . whoever,' he said, convinced that the ache in his heart would never go away. And that he would probably never sleep again.

Risha's lips turned up in a hint of a smile. 'The first time I met you, I really did think you were normal.'

He looked at her in confusion.

'I didn't go out with Dhruv tonight. I had plans to, but I cancelled at the last minute.'

'Why?'

'I didn't think it would be fair to him,' she explained.

'Why not?' he asked, holding his breath.

'Because I'm in love with someone else.'

His heart sank. Was it the Avengers guy?

Arjun cleared his throat and nodded. 'I see.'

Risha held the door wide open and looked up at him, her eyes brimming with laughter. 'Mr Khanna, would you like to come in?'

His heart pounding, Arjun stood in his spot and stared into her bright eyes. 'Why?'

She stepped over the threshold into the corridor and placed a hand on his jaw. 'Because I love you too.'

Arjun inhaled sharply and yanked her forward, slamming his lips down on hers. His kiss was a silent apology, an urgent benediction, an insatiable hunger. Her lips parted eagerly and the kiss became possessive, like he wanted to devour her with his mouth, brand her with his touch.

He crushed her tightly to his chest and said fiercely, 'I love you so much, Risha. And I'm so sorry I hurt you.'

She shook her head. 'I can handle fighting, but I'm not a fan of the silent treatment. You need to start communicating with me, okay?'

He nodded, cupping her face in his hands and kissing her softly.

'Just like that,' she murmured against his lips.

Arjun laughed and rested his chin on her head. 'I missed you.'

'I missed you too,' she said, taking him by the hand and pulling him inside her apartment.

'Are you sure?' Arjun asked.

She nodded.

'What about your parents' rule?'

'It's a silly rule. They're visiting next month and I'm going to propose a revision in all the rules.'

'If I come in,' he warned, 'I may not leave.'

'Why, what do you have in mind?' she teased.

'To be honest,' he confessed, raking a hand through his hair, 'I could really use some sleep.'

'Me too,' she admitted. 'I haven't slept in days.'

Arjun wrapped his arms around her. 'I haven't slept in years.'

Scandal Day 142

3.11 p.m.

Arjun answered his phone with a wide smile. He had been looking forward to this call all day.

'Hello!' he said cheerily.

'What did you say to Nani?' his mother screeched.

'What do you mean?' he asked innocently.

'You're driving to *Patiala*?' she cried.

'Actually, we're driving to Amritsar, but we're stopping over at Patiala and Ludhiana on the way,' Arjun said.

'What do you mean by "we"? Who is this *"we"*?' she shrieked in a thick Punjabi accent.

Arjun muffled a laugh. 'Risha and I.'

Amrita sounded panicked. 'Who is Richa?'

'*Risha* is my girlfriend.'

'Since when do you have a *girlfriend*? And why haven't I met her?!' she yelled.

'Oh, but you have met her,' Arjun drawled.

'No, I haven't!' Amrita said frantically.

'Yes, you have,' he assured her. 'At Chinky's wedding.'

'At Chinky's wedding? Who *is* this girl?' his mother demanded.

Knowing this would definitely push her over the edge, Arjun said with a chuckle, 'The wedding photographer.'

5.37 p.m.

WhatsApp Chat

Risha Kohli: Did you speak to your mom?
Arjun Khanna: Yes.
Risha Kohli: How did it go?

Arjun Khanna: Very well.

Risha Kohli: Liar.

Arjun Khanna: Did you speak to Nani?

Risha Kohli: Yes.

Arjun Khanna: How did it go?

Risha Kohli: Great, as usual. Although, she asked me if I still have the kaleera from Chinky's wedding.

Arjun Khanna: Do you?

Risha Kohli: Of course not.

Arjun Khanna: Liar.

Risha Kohli: She also said something very odd to me.

Arjun Khanna: What did she say?

Risha Kohli: She said, 'Bring thee kaleera with you to Patiala, you can leave it at thee gurdwara here.' Any idea what that's about?

Arjun Khanna: I think she has her heart set on marrying you off to Harinder *'pat name Harry'*.

Risha Kohli: Maybe I *will* marry him.

Arjun Khanna: Maybe you won't.

ACKNOWLEDGEMENTS

My parents—who are responsible for every single thing that's right with me.

My husband—who reads my work much faster than he should and claims it's because I 'write so well'. Thank you for being my sounding board, my punching bag and my Eureka Forbes.

Snigdha and Nikhil—the perfect models for depicting sibling relationships accurately: two parts loyalty, one part humour and one part OCD.

My Urdu-poetry-loving grandfathers and my pure Punjabi grandmothers—for choosing me, out of a dozen grandkids, as their favourite.

My in-laws—for taking pride in all my achievements, no matter how big or small.

My first readers and favourite girls—Nidhi Arora, the left half of my brain, the yang to my yin, and Priyanka Rai, about whom I have a billion wicked thoughts on a daily basis.

Friends, some whose names and others whose personalities I have shamelessly stolen for this book—Kunal Walia, who, despite being away for six months in a year, is always around; Rohan Sehgal, for being my voice of reason and for always answering the phone, irrespective of the time difference; Sameer Walzade of Sonder Frames, for patiently answering my five dozen photography-related questions and five million existential ones; and Jessica Anand Gupta—oh, I think that I've found myself a cheerleader—she is always right there when I need her.

Ekta Rekhi, Mihir Modi and Richa Pandey—for alternately requesting and bribing (but mostly just terrorizing) me to write a book since the day I met them. Can we please move the gun away from my head now?

Diptakirti Chaudhuri—writer par excellence, expert on all things Bollywood, mentor and friend.

Angad B. Sodhi—the 'real' wedding photographer, for shooting the cover! You. Are. Brilliant.

Brinda Kumar and Prashant Verma—if people truly judge books by their covers, you guys made this one a winner.

The brilliant team at Penguin Random House India— unofficially the Fawad Khan fan club, officially the best team I could've asked for: Devangana Dash, Shruti Katoch Dhadwal, Cibani Premkumar and Tarini Uppal. Least, but not last (because *that* is just one error I would make without him), Ambar Sahil Chatterjee—friend first, editor second. Thank you.